Christmas
at
Bar Haven

Also by Phyllis Clark Nichols

THE FAMILY PORTRAIT SERIES
The Christmas Portrait—Book One
The Birthday Portrait—Book Two
The Christmas Portrait Surprise—Book Three

THE ROCKWATER SUITE
Return of the Song—Book One
Freedom of the Song—Book Two
Ransom for a Song—Book Three
Christmas Wedding Song—Book Four
Searching for the Song—Book Five
Springtime of the Song—Book Six

CHRISTMAS BOOKS
Christmas at Grey Sage
Silent Days, Holy Night

NOW AVAILABLE IN AUDIO BOOKS –
Read by Phyllis Clark Nichols
The Christmas Portrait
The Birthday Portrait
Return of the Song
Freedom of the Song
Ransom for a Song
Christmas at Grey Sage
Silent Days, Holy Night

Christmas
at
Bar Haven

Phyllis Clark Nichols

Southern
Stories
Publishing

CHRISTMAS AT BAR HAVEN
Copyright © 2023 by Phyllis Clark Nichols

Published by Southern Stories Publishing

Lyrics to "Sweet Little Jesus Boy" written by Robert MacGimsey (1934).

This is a work of fiction. Names, characters, places, and incidents are products of the author's imagination or used fictitiously. Any similarity to actual people, organizations, and/or events is purely coincidental.

ISBN: 979-8-9888854-0-5 (paperback)
ISBN: 979-8-9888854-1-2 (ebook)
Print Edition

Cover art from an original oil painting by George W. Nichols

In memory

of

Mama,
whose table always had room for one more,
whether it was Tuesday lunch
or Christmas Dinner.

Prologue

---◆---

Near Christmas 2020

My name's Reese. As the oldest son of Stuart and Jillian O'Hara, I grew up right here in Bar Haven in a sprawling old dwelling that has been the roof over three generations of O'Haras.

That longstanding, painted clapboard house is as weathered as my great-grandfather's face, which I've only seen in photographs. I never knew him, but I've heard all the stories. And they were plenty. He was a merchant seaman and spent most of his life at sea, leaving his wife and son here in the house he built with his own hands, sending money and packages from places afar to take care of their needs. Gramps told me the only time he could be certain he would see his father was at Christmas, as the seaman never missed a Christmas at home.

When my gramps became a man, he was determined to make that house a real home for his family. He added on rooms, bathrooms, and a carriage house after the mercantile business he started in town became successful. No seafaring adventures for him. To Gramps, the ocean was only for surf fishing, swimming, and watching the waves. He loved his house and lived there until he died. My uncle got the mercantile business, and my dad got the clapboard house.

The house creeps around a corner lot and is shaded by three live oaks and surrounded by cabbage palmettos, swamp lilies, and the one magnolia tree Gramps planted himself. The salt air isn't always kind to wood. Oh, the paint that timeworn house has seen, all shades of blue and white. Could probably fill a tanker. Growing up, I spent many an hour climbing a ladder with a four-inch-wide paint brush in my hands and the smell of paint mixed with salt air in my lungs. The house was a curious one for my younger brother, Riley, and me. So many rooms and hallways, a secret passageway, the carriage house out back—all connected by stories of three generations before us.

I left home long enough to go to college, but saltwater runs in my veins, and I have a need to wake up to the smell of the marshlands and to the sound of waves and seagulls. So I earned my art degree at the University of North Carolina in Chapel Hill and came home to the Georgia shores as soon as I could.

When I was just a young lad, Gramps bought the old lighthouse out on the point as soon as he heard it was up for sale. The lighthouse hadn't been used in years, but Gramps bought it and kept it up all these years. Somehow I think it tied him to his seafaring father. I was fortunate to build a small cottage and my art studio next to it. Nothing spacious like the old house I grew up in, but it's quiet out here. I can breathe the salt air, and I have plenty of seascapes to paint. Nothing quite like having a cup of coffee in your hand and climbing those steps to view the horizon in the early morning when the coral sun peeps over those deep-blue waves. With the curve of the coastline, Bar Haven is about as protected as it can be from the gale-force winds and high waves, and at low tide I have a bird's-eye view of the sandbar connecting the harbor to the point.

Not much pleases me more than the sensation of smearing paint on a canvas or the breath of the ocean breeze in my hair and the feel of sand underneath my feet. Mama says the point out here is my soul's place—that one place on this whole earth where I really belong. Where I am truly alive until I go to heaven. She says everyone has a place like that.

Late every afternoon, I take my ritual climb up the stairs of the lighthouse and stare out at the horizon. The ocean seems alive. The breezes are its breath, and that steady lapping where the water meets the land is its heartbeat. It sings to me. I know I am blessed to do what I love in my sacred space, that place where all of life comes together for me. It took a while, but I make a good living painting the ever-changing skies and water of this coastline. Collectors find my work in galleries up and down the coasts of Georgia, Florida, and South Carolina.

My parents still live in that clapboard house, and I've already given it a fresh coat of paint this year. I went by for a visit last Sunday, and Mama's gathering room looked like someone had dumped last year's Christmas on those weathered wood floors. Actually, it wasn't only last year's Christmas but nearly two decades of Christmases. Now Mama had already decorated the eight-foot fir in front of the picture window in the living room. She always says that tree's for the townsfolk to see when they amble down the sidewalk.

But no one decorates what Mama calls the family tree until all her little birds return to the nest the weekend after Christmas.

All of Bar Haven is getting ready for Christmas next Friday, and I'm about to close up the studio for a couple of weeks. But I have one last job to do. Something that should have been done seventeen years ago. I can't quite figure why it hasn't already been done.

Now, I've never wanted for anything to paint. A blank canvas or a piece of watercolor paper has never frightened me. I've never had a creative block. Never been too mentally exhausted to put a swipe of paint on paper. But this Christmas ornament Mama asked me to paint has me stumped. I've stared at this plain glass Christmas ball most of the morning, and I have not one inkling or impression of what to put on it in spite of all my memories. Maybe I should sleep on it, and tomorrow it'll come.

Next Sunday, on December 27, besides Riley and his family and me, there'll be twelve of Mama's other little birds coming from all directions to put our special Christmas ornaments on the Scotch pine tree by the fireplace in the kitchen. Through the years, Mama made an ornament for each of her little birds—that is, for each of us except Johanna.

And this is her story.

Chapter One

—◆—

Late January 2003
Seawalk Pavilion,
Jacksonville, Florida

With the sun setting behind them, John and Anna Beth sat under the palm tree on the beach and watched the glistening gold of the waves gently kiss the shore. The January breezes were cooler than usual, but the beach was their place to be together. She inched closer to him and pulled the blanket more tightly around her shoulders, feeling his arm around her.

"Are you sure this is the best plan, John? I have some money saved. We can use that."

"No, that's your money for school. And no, I'm not sure, but I think it is. The thing I *am* sure of is how much I love you, and I want us to have a good life, and this is the surest way I can see for now. But I don't like being away from you. I'm hoping they'll let me off a few days so I can come back for your graduation."

She felt his gentle squeeze on her shoulder. "I don't know if I can bear it, John. And you leave next week?"

"Yep." He grew quiet for a moment, and then in a melancholy voice, he said, "But I promise I'll email you every day, and I'll call when I can."

She knew John was rock solid, but still her stomach became uneasy. His promise echoed the promise her father had made the day he packed his bags and walked out on her and her mother. Not because he needed to go, like John did, but because he wanted to. She was only six, but she'd never forgotten the sight and sound of him slamming the front porch door and yelling as he walked away with a stuffed duffle bag. He never called, and he never returned.

Since he left, her life for the last twelve years had been a revolving door of her mother's boyfriends and her rebounding from jobs and layoffs. The only predictable thing in Anna Beth's life had been uncertainty. Books had become her refuge. As an above-average student despite the absence of any encouragement, she would be graduating in May, and her plan was to go to college. She would make something of herself.

Anna Beth wanted to be a nurse. She could not remember a time when she didn't want to be a nurse. Even in pigtails, she had wrapped bandages on stray cats and massaged her mother's feet at the end of her shift at the 7-Eleven. Her heart was at home when she was taking care of hurts and boo-boos. When the guidance counselor at her high school had given her information about a community college that offered a course of study that would license her to be an LPN in approximately a year, her hope ignited her determination. Knowing there would be no help for college from her mom, she took a part-time job as a clerk at a local supermarket during her junior year. She had saved over three thousand dollars in a year and a half. Three thousand dollars that she kept secret from her mother.

But the best thing about her job was that she had met John. He was twenty-one and the produce manager.

"I guess you're right. By the time you get home in September, I'll be almost halfway through getting my LPN license. And by early next year, I should be working in a hospital and making good money."

"And I'll be home and have money for us to get married and have a nice place to live. Just think, Anna Beth, by Christmas we could be married. It would be the very best Christmas of my life. I can get a steady job as a welder and go to technical school and get my license to be an electrician. Lucky for me I can weld. It means I'll get good pay on that oil rig, too, and I can send you money to help, especially with school and all."

"You don't need to do that. I think I have it covered. I just want you to hurry up and get home."

"I'm hoping the time'll pass quickly. I mean, I'll be working every day—e-ver-y day—on an oil rig in the middle of the Gulf of Mexico. That's a lot of water." He paused. "I want to come home to watch you walk across that stage and get your diploma. I don't know if my supervisor will allow it, but I'm gonna try. Just in case, I have something special planned Friday night. We don't have to wait until your graduation to celebrate."

"You don't have to do that. I just want to spend as much time with you as I can before you leave next week."

He forced a chuckle. "Me too." He then became quiet, and she felt him twirling her blond curls around his finger. "Anna Beth. We're going to have a good life, better than what we've known, aren't we? I mean, we'll be together, and we're getting our education like Miss Edith said. Then we can have a house and a family. And I'll take care of you and make you smile every day."

"I cannot wait, John. My dreams are coming true. I'll be your wife, and I'll be a nurse."

He had told her stories about his childhood, which had been harder than hers. Her father just left, but John's father led with his left and followed with his right. Out of fear for their lives, his mom had taken John and left Savannah.

They didn't have money to get far. They'd hoped Jacksonville was distant enough to start a new life, just the two of them—a life where they felt safe. And they did well and were happy for a while before his mom got sick. Breast cancer. At sixteen, John had dropped out of school to take care of her until she died a year later. Returning to school did not seem an option to him, so he kept his job as a stockboy at the local supermarket. Miss Edith, one of the clerks there and a church-going lady, took him under her wing. She fed him, invited him to church, and tutored him to get his GED. He was a responsible worker, and after a year the owner of the supermarket made him the produce manager, but John had other interests. Miss Edith's husband was a welder, and he took John on as an apprentice. Welding was the skill that had gotten him a job on an oil rig in the Gulf of Mexico. A nine-month contract.

Anna Beth felt her tears coming. "You're already talking about the best Christmas of your life, and I'm wondering how I'll make it without you until you get home."

John stood, brushed the sand off his hands. He took her hand, pulled her up to him, and gently kissed her forehead. His voice became low and sweet. "Here's how we'll make it. When I'm really missing you, I'll close my eyes, and I'll see you in our little cottage. The Christmas tree will be shining in the window, and you'll be standing at the front door waiting for me, standing under the mistletoe. And I'll remember how it feels to take you in my arms just like it feels right now."

Anna Beth smiled from the inside out amid her tears. "And I'll do the same thing. I'll think about our first Christmas. I'll be standing in the doorway waiting for you to come through the gate. And I'll remember how your arms feel around me."

———·———

A few days later

Anna Beth stood on the stoop and fidgeted as she waited for Miss Edith to answer the door. She looked at her mom's dilapidated car parked out front on the street. It stood out among the other sedans parked up and down this neighborhood. She dreamed about living in a neighborhood like this, in a bungalow like Miss Edith's, and driving a car with no dents and a shiny paint job.

The door creaked as Miss Edith opened it. "Well, Anna Beth, get yourself in here. And what are you doing coming to the front door? Not even the pastor comes to this door."

Anna Beth stepped in, and Miss Edith closed the creaking door. "Need to send Harry around here to grease these hinges." She took Anna Beth's arm and talked as she walked. "So, tell me, you got John off today?"

"I'll remember next time about the door, Miss Edith. And, yes, ma'am. I didn't go to school today so I could take him to the airport. He had a flight at noon. But I'll go to work this afternoon. It'll get my mind off missing John. But the supermarket might make me miss him even more. He's always there."

They walked through the small living room that smelled of stale lavender and down the hallway to the sunporch.

"Let's sit out here, child. It is one gorgeous day. The

Lord knew I needed warm weather, and He planted me in Florida. He knew I get chilled if it gets below seventy degrees, and it's just sixty-six today. But the warm sunshine coming through these windows heats the room and my old bones. Have a seat. Can I get you anything?"

Anna Beth sat in the wicker chair next to shelving lined with African violets. "No, ma'am, but thank you. You must really have a green thumb. Your little flowers look better than ever."

"Oh yes, those violets are my babies. I couldn't have real babies, so I took to growing violets. They get better care than most of the children around here. Been growing them for years, and never did a one of them break my heart. Some of these delicate wonders are older than you, girl, and they can last up to fifty years if I take care of them." Miss Edith chuckled. "And I never bought but three of them. I have friends at church that grow them, too, and we share cuttings and grow our own. Every one of those violets has a name, and it's the name of the friend who gave me the cutting. I talk to them, too, especially when I water them."

Miss Edith paused. "So, what do think about my new étagère?" She sat down on the cushioned wicker sofa underneath the windows.

Anna Beth froze in embarrassment. "Uh, your new . . ."

"That's all right. I didn't know what an étagère was either until that wanna-be-fancy lady at the furniture store called it that. It's just glass shelving. Don't know why she couldn't just say so, but then she probably couldn't have charged me as much for three glass shelves on a chrome stand. I think it looks good out here, and it gives me plenty of space to add some more violets."

"Yes, ma'am. It sure does."

"Can I get you somethin' to snack on since you're going to work? I just bought a whole quart of fresh strawberries.

Aren't we glad we live in Florida and can get the best, juiciest, sweetest strawberries ever, even in the wintertime?"

"Yes, ma'am. I do love strawberries, but maybe I'll have some another time. I can't stay too long. My mom's waiting on her car. She needs it to get to work tonight. I've had it all day to get John to the airport." She hesitated. "I can't believe I may not see him until October, but he said he'd try to come home for a few days for my graduation."

She reached into the straw bag she was carrying and pulled out an envelope. "John wanted me to give you this." She was careful to extend the envelope with her left hand.

Miss Edith reached for the envelope, but before she took it, she looked at Anna Beth and let out a loud chuckle. "Oh, honey child, you didn't come by to bring me this envelope. You came by to show me what's on that beautiful little hand of yours."

Anna Beth's smile filled her face. "Yes ma'am, I did. John and I are engaged, but no one else knows, not even my mom. We wanted you to be the first to know."

"Well, tell me all about it. Your blond curls are as bouncy as ever, but your blue eyes tell a different story. I know you must feel like I did when Harry left me and joined the marines. I thought I would die before I saw him again. Never been so sad in my life. Your eyes look like mine did. But my, you really have something special to look forward to."

"Yes, ma'am. We haven't missed one day of seeing each other since I started working at the supermarket last year. I don't know how I'll be, missing him so much. I've never really missed anybody except my daddy before." Anna Beth settled back in the wicker chair.

She watched Miss Edith put the envelope on the wicker table in front of the sofa. "You'll be just fine. Oh, you'll miss him, but you have school, and work every day after school, and you'll be graduating here before you know it. And you kids have email and cellphones. Harry and I had to write letters and use payphones. Why, I wore out a pair of shoes walking to the mailbox every day for the three months he was in basic training. But we made it. Still making it after forty-six years."

"Yes, ma'am. That's what I want more than anything. We're going to get married, stay happy, and stay married. I know I have a lot to learn, but I want to be a good wife like you are. John is such a good man, and he deserves someone to love him and take care of him."

"Yes, he does. And you're just the perfect one for him. I know he loves you, girl. You're both real young, and you two have had some hard knocks that made you grow up a little faster than most, but you're making a choice to do life differently. No need to repeat those old behaviors that don't make for a happy home."

"No, ma'am." Anna Beth hesitated and then asked, "Are you going to open the envelope?"

"Eventually. But first I want to hear about how John proposed. So tell me."

"Well, John told me to dress up like I was going to church and he would pick me up at seven. I thought we were celebrating my graduation in case he doesn't get to come home for it. Anyway, we went to this fancy restaurant over at the harbor. He asked for a table next to the window so we could watch the boats come in."

"Uh-huh. Tell me how he asked you."

"We had this wonderful dinner of shrimp and scallops, and then he ordered cheesecake for dessert. It was a fancy meal. One of those places with fresh flowers on the table. Then we took a walk along the harbor and stopped under the streetlight. A cruise ship was docking, and it was lit up like Christmas." Anna Beth took a deep breath. "While we were watching, John said, 'What would you think about taking a cruise for our honeymoon?' Now, Miss Edith, we had talked about getting married and my going to college to be a nurse and about all our dreams, but he'd never just outright asked me to marry him. I just liked talking and thinking about marrying him."

"I see, and that's kind of normal." Miss Edith waited.

"Then John got down on one knee and pulled this ring out of his shirt pocket." Anna Beth twisted the ring on her finger. "Then he said, 'I suppose I should ask you to marry me before we plan our honeymoon. Anna Beth Nelson, will you make me the happiest man on earth and say yes to becoming my wife?' I thought I would faint."

"Well, our John did it up right. And that ring looks mighty sweet on that little hand of yours."

"It was his mother's, and she gave it to him before she died and told him to save it until he found the woman that would make his heart whole."

"Now his mama's ring makes it even more special."

"Yes, ma'am. We want to get married in October as soon as he gets home. John really wants us to be married and living in our house for our first Christmas. I'll still be in nursing school, but I'll marry him on the first day he returns if that's what he wants."

"Oh no. You and John will set a date, and I'll help you plan the wedding. You can have it in our little church. All the folks there just love you and John." Miss Edith leaned her head back. "A wedding. Now that's something to really look forward to."

"Are you going to read the letter, Miss Edith?"

"Well, Anna Beth, the letter is for me. Could I read it first? And then, if I think John wouldn't mind, I'll let you read it."

"Oh yes, ma'am, I'd really like that."

Miss Edith opened the envelope and read the note that was handwritten in pencil on a ruled page torn from a notebook. She took her time. Anna Beth watched her expressions change as she read silently, only allowing an *oh my* or an *aww* to quietly escape her lips. Anna Beth could feel her own heart beating. She had wanted to open the envelope herself, but she'd done what John asked her to do.

Miss Edith looked up at her. "I think John wouldn't mind at all if you read this letter. It surely tells you what kind of man he is." She handed the letter to Anna Beth.

Anna Beth's hands trembled, and she bit her lip as she read.

Dear Miss Edith,

I wish I could have said these words to your face, but somehow, I just couldn't. I'm going away for nine months, so I won't be around to mow your grass and eat those fine pineapple sandwiches you make. I will miss you and Mr. Harry. Y'all are the closest things to family I ever had. For the last five years, you have fed me. You made sure I got my GED, and then Mr. Harry taught me welding. Without the two of you, I wouldn't have this good job, and I couldn't ask Anna Beth to marry me. I want to say thank you for everything, and I mean everything, you have done for me. You believed in me when nobody else did.

I'll be missing Anna Beth, and I think she'll be missing me. I was writing to say thank you and to ask you to look out for her while I'm gone. She'll be going to school and working, but I don't want her to be lonely. I'll write and call her, and I'll write and call you, too, but I was hoping you could check in on her sometimes. I've asked her to marry me. I know she'll tell you all about that. I was hoping you could help her plan a little wedding. Nothing real fancy, but I'll pay for everything. I want us to get married in the church. No justice of the peace for us. If you could do that one thing, I surely would appreciate it, Miss Edith.

One more thing. Tell whoever is mowing your grass to put out that special fertilizer I left in the shed in April and again in June. I'll be back to fertilize your grass come October. I love you, Miss Edith. Now I'm going off to earn some money and come back and make you proud.

Love,

John

Anna Beth breathed deeply, wiped her eyes with the backs of her hands, and looked up. "That's our John, Miss Edith." She held up the letter like she was preaching from the gospel book. "This is why we love him so." She stood from her chair. "Now, I'd best be getting home and then to work. John said he might call me when he gets settled in Houston tonight."

Chapter Two

---◆---

Middle of March 2003
Bar Haven, on the coast of Georgia

It was an early Thursday morning during the week of spring break. Twelve-year-old Reese gathered the loose papers from his drafting table. Lucky for him that his second-floor bedroom was flooded with light from every direction except the north, and it was spacious enough to accommodate the large, antique drafting table, a gift from his gramps when he'd learned that Reese spent so much time drawing and doing watercolors.

He had begged his mama months ago to remove all the curtains and shades covering the large windows. Now the only window coverings hung over the north windows facing the street. His mother had insisted on keeping those. Reese craved the light that poured through the wavy old panes and through the mason jars of colored pencils and paint brushes lining the windowsills on the eastern side of the house.

He shuffled the pages of drawings then froze, looking

straight at the door, and let out his signature whistle. His gramps had taught him to whistle like that. It was a signal for Riley, his four-year-old brother whose room was down the hall. Sometimes it was a friendly let's-get-going whistle. Today, it was not.

"Riley, get yourself in here now." He stepped to the door. "Riley, I know you heard me. Get yourself in here *now!*" He stepped back to the bed and began checking his projector bag. He reached for a fist full of charcoal pencils on the table and put them in the side pocket of his bag.

Riley came to the door. "I'm here, Reese. Dad says we need to come downstairs. He's almost ready to go."

"Not until you tell me what you did with my camel drawing. I know you took it."

Riley squirmed and stalled. He rubbed the red curls on his head, and his eyes shifted from side to side. "Uh, you can't find your picture of the camel?"

"No, I cannot find my drawing. What did you do with it? I know you had it."

"Did not." Riley spoke quietly, stalling.

"Don't you be fibbing. You know what Mama says about fibbing."

Riley stood as still as the cast-iron statue of the mermaid next to the garden pool out back. Only his eyeballs rolled around as though he was searching the entire room and the inside of his brain simultaneously for the drawing of the camel. "I remember. It's in the carriage house."

Reese turned to look at his brother. "The carriage house? What's it doing in the carriage house? If you don't find it, I'm going to tie you to one of the highest rafters in that carriage house." He looked at Riley, still frozen in the doorway. "Go. Get out of here. We can't leave until you find it."

Reese finished packing up his gear, and Riley was

bounding back into the room in less than two minutes, almost breathless and holding a damp piece of paper. "I found it."

Reese took it. "Riley . . . Riley, I'm going to—"

"No, Reese. I found it."

"Yeah, it's wet. It's ruined."

"You can dry it. Mama can put it in the dryer. That's what she does when my shirt gets wet."

Reese held it up to the light of the window. "What were you doing in the carriage house with my drawing?"

Riley hedged before answering. "Jake came over yesterday to play, and we were building a fort in the carriage house. I told him about all your drawings and the camel with two humps. Jake said camels have only one hump, and I told him your camel had two. He didn't believe me. And I just wanted to show him. I just wanted to—"

"Then why didn't you *just* ask me? And why didn't you *just* bring it back?"

"I meant to, Reese." Riley hesitated. "I think I forgot."

"You think? Now what am I going to do? Dad's waiting on me, and my drawing of the camel is ruined. You're in big trouble with me and Dad now." Reese picked up his duffle bag and swished by his brother. "Come on, Riley. Take it like a man."

Riley ran around his brother and took the lead down the stairs, yelling as he went. "Dad, I'm not in trouble. I just forgot. You forget sometimes. I promise I just forgot."

Sitting in his chair at the breakfast table, Stuart O'Hara folded the newspaper and looked at his young son. "And what is it that you forgot, Riley?"

Before Riley could speak, Reese held up the wet paper. "He didn't just forget. He took my drawing without my permission and then left it in the carriage house. How it got so wet, I don't know. But Dad, I think it's ruined. We won't be able to get the camel done today."

His dad turned in his chair to Riley, who stood at his side. "And so you took Reese's drawing without asking and forgot to return it? And pray tell, how did it get wet? Or did you forget that too?"

"Jake wouldn't believe me that a camel has two humps. I had to show him, and it . . . it just flew outta my hands and landed in the goldfish pool out back. But I got it."

"Um-huh. It just flew out of your hands, and you failed to let anybody know about it." His dad put his hands on Riley's shoulders. "Son, your brother worked hard on that picture, and we're supposed to be at Mr. Buckingham's workshop in fifteen minutes for Reese to project that drawing onto a large piece of plywood. And then, out of the goodness of his heart, Mr. Buckingham agreed to cut the camel out for Reese to paint. Did you forget that Reese is helping us make the life-sized animals for the live nativity at Christmas?"

Riley shook his head. "A wooden camel isn't alive."

"You'd be right about that. But real live camels and sheep are hard to come by in this little coastal town. So we're doing the best we can. And now, because of you, Reese's drawing is ruined, and I must call Mr. Buckingham and tell him we're not coming."

His mother came from the kitchen. "Let me see the drawing, son."

Reese handed her the damp paper. "It's ruined, Mama."

"Well, maybe not. It's just a bit damp. Give me five minutes." She took the drawing and walked out of the room.

While she was gone, his dad continued his conversation with young Riley about the importance of being responsible. His brother seemed to have a "But, Dad" every time Stuart took a breath. "No more *buts*, Riley," their father finally said. "This isn't about forgetting. It's about taking something that doesn't belong to you. What do you think would be an appropriate punishment that would help you remember not to do that?"

Standing in his tracks, Riley twisted back and forth and blurted out. "I think you should make me draw a picture of a camel. No, two pictures. A camel with one hump and another camel with two humps like Reese's."

Reese dropped his duffle bag to the floor and sat down at the table with his dad. "Well, just maybe you could draw one good enough for Mr. Buckingham to use." He looked at the kitchen clock above the porch door. "And make that in fifteen minutes."

His father looked at Reese. "Reese, how much time did you spend drawing that camel?"

Reese thought for a minute. "Maybe a couple of hours or a little more. But Dad, I had to do research. This was the kind of camel the Wise Men rode to see Jesus. That's why this camel had two humps. Then I spent time practicing other sketches before I drew this one."

"Do you think two hours in time-out in his room might be adequate for Riley?"

Still wanting to tie his little brother to the rafters in the carriage house, he finally muttered. "I guess so. But he can't be playing. He's got to do something that he doesn't like to do. He can't just sit in there and play or have Jake over."

His father almost chuckled. "You mean like brushing his teeth or combing his hair? What would you like him to do?"

Before Reese could answer, his mother returned with a dry and flat drawing of a Bactrian camel. "Get out your charcoal pencil, Reese. I think your camel just might return if you darkened these lines."

Reese reached for his duffle bag. "How did you do that, Mama?"

"A hot iron can do more than press your dad's shirts."

He took the paper, and within minutes the drawing had been restored. "No need to call Mr. Buckingham, Dad. I think I can project this and then sketch it onto the plywood. We're good to go."

Riley clapped his hands. "Okay, I'm ready. Let's go."

His father stood from his chair and rubbed Riley's red curls. "I think you forgot something else. You're not going with us. You're going up to your room for the next two hours and see if you can stay out of trouble. Your brother has spent several hours during his spring break from school getting these drawings ready, and you nearly ruined this one. I don't think you're responsible enough yet to be in Mr. Buckingham's workshop." He turned his younger son around and pointed to the stairs. "Now, go. Your mother will check on you. But use this time to think about what you've done and how many people were affected—or nearly affected—by it."

———•———

Stuart drove the back streets to Mr. Buckingham's workshop while Reese sorted his drawings one more time, deciding which to draw first.

"You have them all ready, son?"

"Yes, sir. Thanks to Mama. She came to our rescue with that iron."

"Seems like your mother is always coming to someone's rescue, mostly ours. She and Mrs. Franklin are really putting their efforts into this live nativity project. Lots of church folks getting involved already. A boat builder constructing the frame. Several of the ladies making costumes. And it's only March. Your mother says that getting people involved and excited about it all through the year might be the best thing that happens."

"Mama's good at getting people to do stuff." He put the papers back in the side pocket of his bag. "I have the drawings for the camel, a donkey, one sheep lying down and another standing, and one cow. I know Mama didn't request this, but also I have a picture of a dove. I thought we could put him on the rafter in the manger. I saw one in a painting I studied while I was doing the drawings. It's symbolic, you know. I read it was the symbol of peace and God's presence."

Stuart stopped at the traffic light. "That gives me a great idea. Why don't you do two more of those doves. One for the nativity scene and two for your mama for Christmas. You know how she loves her birds, and this one would be her special keepsake for the first live nativity. It would be even more special since you drew and painted it."

Reese smiled, wishing he had thought of that. "Yes, sir, if Mr. Buckingham doesn't mind and he has time."

"I'll take care of that." Stuart pulled into the wide driveway and parked next to a truck, the bed of it filled with sheets of plywood. "Looks like Buck's already picked up the plywood. Probably waiting on us to help him get it out of the truck.

Charles Buckingham, known as Buck to the townsfolk, came through the open double doors of his workshop wearing his shop apron and brushing sawdust from his gray beard. "A hearty morning to you O'Hara men. Right on time to provide some muscle for unloading that plywood."

Stuart shook Buck's hand. Reese pulled his bag from the floorboard of the car and took it inside before he returned to the truck to help.

They unloaded quickly. Reese then set up his projector and laid the drawing of the small sheep on the table. He figured that was the smallest and he could get it drawn on the board in charcoal the quickest. Then Mr. Buckingham could start cutting while he finished the others. "Dad, can you get the plywood propped against the table? Then I can position my projector over this drawing to get the right size."

Mr. Buckingham stood next to Reese and pulled at his beard. "So, tell me, young man, how do you know it'll be the right size?"

Reese pulled a tablet out of his bag and opened it. "I did the research, sir. I have the actual sizes of all the animals right here. We will make them life sized, just like Mama wants. Except for the camel and the cow. They're just too big." He looked at his dad. "Did you bring the measuring tape?"

He knew the answer when he saw his dad's face.

"I'm afraid with Riley's mess this morning, I forgot it. Buck, you must have a measuring tape around here somewhere."

Buck chuckled. "How many do you need?"

Within a few minutes, Reese had finished his sketch of a small reclining sheep on the piece of plywood, and Buck took it to his band saw like he'd been waiting to do this job all his life. He put in his ear plugs and cautioned Stuart to stand back. In less than five minutes, a wooden likeness of a sheep appeared.

He walked over to Reese, who was drawing the donkey. "Now, Reese, tell me again—why we aren't we getting a life-sized camel and cow?"

"The camel's pretty big, sir. Like ten to twelve feet from nose to rump and up to six feet high."

Buck scratched his beard again. "We got hinges, boy. No miniature camel or cow for our nativity scene. Three sheets of plywood and we got ourselves a real life-sized camel. I already figured we need to put these animals together in pieces and hinge them, or else I'll get the what-fors from the preacher's wife when she goes to store them in the church attic after Christmas. Better for moving them around, anyway, I think. Hinges going to be a problem for painting?"

"No, sir. No problem. And I can do that life-sized camel, Mr. Buckingham, but I'll have to move this projector way back. And like you said, it'll take three sheets of your plywood. Do you have enough?"

"I believe I do, and if I don't, I know where to get some right quick like." He patted Reese on the back. "Christmas is a long way off. But it's a fine young man who would give up part of his spring break to work so hard on this project, especially with an old man like me. You make your daddy proud, and your old grandfather would be mighty proud too. He's probably looking down from heaven right now wondering why we're making such a fuss over Christmas in March."

Reese felt his face grow red and his heart a little sad thinking about his gramps. "Thank you, sir. But I enjoy drawing and painting. So it's not like work to me."

They worked steadily until Reese finished the last drawing and put his projector away. He walked over to watch Buck cut the last pieces of the camel.

Buck finished the last cut and brushed the sawdust away from the board. "All done." He moved the piece from his saw to the floor. "Nothing like the smell of fresh sawdust. Just makes me feel good."

Reese smiled knowingly. "I understand, sir. The smell of paint makes me feel the same way. And this project means lots of paint and new brushes. I'll be back tomorrow to start the painting, if that's all right with you."

"I'll be here and waiting to see you work your magic."

Stuart put the broom back in the corner closet. "Thank

you, Buck. Sorry I'm not much help in the shop, and I sure can't paint, but I'm a master at sweeping up sawdust. We'll be on our way and see you tomorrow." He turned to Reese. "Let's go, son."

———.———

Jillian quietly pushed open the door to Riley's room. Her son lay on his bed going through his baseball cards. "Riley?"

He jumped up flat-footed on the bed in a flash. "Yes, ma'am. I've thought about what I did, and I'm real sorry. And I really mean it, Mama. Can I go outside now?"

She walked over to the bed and motioned for him. He stepped across the bed into her arms. She held him close and spoke softly. "I'm glad that you're sorry, Riley. Saying you're sorry and meaning it are just more signs you're growing up. What am I to do when you're too big to jump on the bed and hug my neck?"

Riley giggled. "I'll be getting big. But I'll always hug your neck."

"I'm counting on it." She ran her fingers through his red curls. "You know, Riley, maybe you could apologize to your brother when he gets home and ask him to forgive you."

"I will, Mama. I promise. And I'll say it like I mean it, 'cause I really do." He pulled away from her. "Is it time I can get out of here and go outside and play?"

"Well, not exactly. You can leave your room, but I have a job you can help me with. It's threatening rain, and I don't want you outside. Put your shoes on. I have your morning snack ready downstairs, and then you can go out to the carriage house and help me."

"What are we going to do?"

"I'd like a little help with cleaning up the apartment upstairs over the carriage house. And I have a couple of jobs you can do."

"Huh? Gramps doesn't live there anymore. He's in heaven. Why do you clean his apartment?"

When Stuart's mother died, Jillian and Stuart had been living in a small cottage across town. Stuart's father had invited them to come live in his big house, saying he would take the upstairs carriage apartment out back. He'd have his own space, yet his family would be steps away. He had outfitted the apartment with a kitchen, bath, two bedrooms, a balcony porch, and a living area. Jillian really missed him. He was always a joy, and he had been such help with the boys. After he died last year, she'd put it on her schedule to go out to the apartment a couple of times a month to freshen up the space—to dust, vacuum, clean the bathroom, and wipe down the kitchen counters. She couldn't explain her reasoning to herself, much less to five-year-old Riley.

"Are you keeping it clean for Gramps?" Riley asked as they walked out to the carriage house. "You think he's coming back?"

"No, Riley. He's happy in heaven. I just like things clean." She was telling the truth—as much of the truth as he could understand.

They had finished cleaning and were standing on the small, covered porch of the apartment, watching the rain shower, when Stuart and Reese drove in. Stuart parked the car and grabbed an umbrella out of the back seat and called to them on his way up the stairs. "I see a damsel in distress, and I'm on my way." He walked up to the steps to the apartment, took Riley in his arms, and covered them all with his umbrella as they walked through the puddled garden to the house.

Jillian held his arm tightly. "Such chivalry."

Stuart looked down at her and grinned. "Not really. Reese and I are hungry, and neither of us is much good in the kitchen. I couldn't leave you out there in the rain and have us fix our own lunch."

"Lunch is in the oven and should be on the table in ten minutes." Jillian was always the happiest when she was taking care of her family and their home.

The smell of meatloaf wrapped in bacon filled the kitchen. With everyone washed up and standing at their places at the table, Stuart seated Jillian, and then they all sat down. After he said grace, Jillian turned to Riley. "Before we eat, I think Riley has something he'd like to say to you, Reese."

Riley fumbled for words, and then they tumbled out. "Yeah, Reese. I'm sorry. I thought about it. I shoulda asked you if it was okay to show Jake the picture. I a-lop . . . a-lop . . ."

His mother rescued him. "The word is *apologize*, Riley. *Apologize*."

Riley nodded his head. "Okay. I *alopogize*, Reese. I won't do it again. I won't never take your drawings without asking you."

Unwilling to correct his double negatives, Jillian smiled and nodded at Riley, showing her pleasure.

Reese responded. "I accept your *alopogy*, brother."

Jillian winked at Stuart and tried to hide her grin. "Okay, boys, let's eat."

Chapter Three

Late March
Jacksonville, Florida

It was late Thursday morning and Anna Beth was still in bed, not feeling well enough to go to school. That was odd for one who'd had perfect attendance for four years.

Her mother, Gina, bumbled into her room dragging a suitcase.

"You still not feeling good?" Before Anna Beth could reply, Gina added, "I didn't have time to do my laundry yesterday. Lucky for me we're about the same size. I need to borrow a few things." She lifted her suitcase to Anna Beth's bed and started grabbing clothes from Anna Beth's closet and chest of drawers, leaving a trail of pieces she'd dropped on the floor. She continued stuffing the borrowed items into her suitcase while she talked. "Anna Beth, you'll be better in no time. It's just a twenty-four-hour virus. You'll be well tomorrow. If you're not better, just call Alicia. She'll come over. I cannot keep Rodney waiting. He wants to get to

Hilton Head before dark to set up the camper."

"I'll be fine, Mom. Don't worry. Take your trip. Just leave me some clothes, please." *And don't worry about those on the floor. I'll pick them up.*

Having been in bed in misery all morning, Anna Beth wasn't so sure she would be fine. She hadn't felt well for several days but had managed to take care of herself. Her mom had been either working all day or at Rodney's all night anyway. So, what difference would her leaving for Hilton Head make?

Now eighteen, she was relieved that Social Services was no longer a threat. She'd lived a childhood of threats. First it was her father's abuse. Fear of his angry outbursts had left scars, but at least his threats left when he slammed the front door for the last time and walked out of their lives for good. But her mother's neglect the last eleven years had kept Anna Beth on the edge of wondering when her mom would return home or when she herself would be taken away by Children's Protective Services. Always the threat of something.

"When are you coming back?"

"I don't know exactly. I've already told you that. Rodney's looking for a new job, and he wants me to go with him. I left a few cans of soup and a box of soda crackers on the kitchen counter. There may still be some orange juice in the fridge. Like I told you, you'll be fine."

"I know I'll be fine, Mom, but how long will it take Rodney to find a job? A couple of days or a week? And what if he finds a new job? What are you planning to do?"

Gina picked up Anna Beth's good hairbrush from the dresser and waved it in the air, pointing it at Anna Beth before tossing it into her bag. "How many times do I have to tell you I don't know? I'll be back when I get back, but I'll call, or you can call me. I just can't miss this trip, Sugar Pie. Rodney has taken a real shine to me. And besides, you'll be gone yourself in another few months, off to school and marrying John. I don't want to be left here all alone."

Neither do I when I feel like my insides are revolting. Nursing school and marrying John can't come soon enough.

Anna Beth was weary of being daughter and parent. And with John, for once in her life, she would have someone to take care of her heart. She mustered enough energy to sit up in the bed. "Are you leaving money to pay the rent next week in case you're not back in time?"

"Oh, you little fusspot, don't worry about the rent. Everything'll be fine."

Everything was always fine for her mom. Her mom never had to worry because Anna Beth had always done the fretting. She was the one who opened the past-due notices and stacked them on the kitchen counter with a note. And more than once, to avoid eviction in the last year, she had paid the rent out of her supermarket earnings.

Gina zipped up the suitcase and pulled it off the bed. "I gotta go, Sugar Pie. I'd hug you, but I really don't want to catch whatever bug you have. I just cannot to be sick on this trip. It's going to be like a vacation." Gina waved and walked out of the bedroom. "Love you."

"Love you, too, Mom." Anna Beth fell back on the bed, limp as a used beach towel, her head buried in the ragged pillow. She whispered, "You're not really coming back, are you?"

She was grateful her mom had stopped bringing her men friends around after one of her drunken visitors had made a nasty scene when Anna Beth was only fourteen. Gina's taste in men was like her choices for a steady diet of fast food, junk food, and crap out of a can. Nothing that was real and healthy and good for you. But her mom said Rodney was different. He had been over a couple of times but never for overnight. He seemed all right, even normal.

Anna Beth hoped he was different like her mom said he was.

She lay in bed, thinking about John and how fortunate she was that he was the real deal and that he loved her. She stared at the small diamond on her ring finger and put forth enough effort to smile. Daydreaming about their talks and walks on the beach and finding a cottage near the beach where they would live happily after they were married, she drifted off to sleep.

Hours later, she woke when her cell rang. She fumbled through the bedcovers searching for the phone. *Missed call.* She recognized Alicia's number and called her back.

"Hey, Alicia."

"Missed you at school today. Are you still sick?" Alicia sounded like she was in a hurry.

Anna Beth looked at the clock on the dresser. Three thirty. She sat up in the bed. "Good grief, I'm glad you called. I was asleep, and I need to be at work in thirty minutes. I didn't feel so well this morning, but I think I feel better now."

"Oh, good. I have your assignments if you'd like to pick them up tonight after work."

"That would be great. Can you stay over with me? Mom left on a trip with Rodney this morning, and she'll be gone for a few days." *Or maybe forever. Who knows?*

"I'll have to ask Mom. Either way, I'll see you after your work. I need to go. Mom has a meeting at the church, and I have to babysit my brother."

"Sure. I'll be by your house a little after eight."

"See you then."

"Later." Anna Beth eased to the side of the bed and sat up, holding her head in her hands, and trying to muster up enough strength to walk to the bathroom. Her head feeling like a whirligig in a March wind, she walked carefully, finally reaching the bathroom. She grabbed the sink for stability and looked at herself in the mirror. Her naturally blond hair was a mess, and her mom had taken her good brush. Pale cheeks. Dark circles under her blue eyes. She hadn't eaten anything since the piece of toast at breakfast nine hours ago. No time to heat the soup her mom had left. She'd find something at the supermarket, maybe a fresh sandwich from the deli and a carton of chocolate milk, her favorite from childhood. It was the only sweet remembrance she had of her father. It was always his peace offering after his episodes.

At least her father had known it was her favorite. Her mom never seemed to remember.

———•———

Anna Beth arrived five minutes early to work, just enough time to grab a sandwich and the last carton of chocolate milk in the refrigerated case. She waved at Miss Edith on her way in. Anna Beth's job was to take over at the cash register at four o'clock when Miss Edith finished her eight-hour shift. This job was perfect for Anna Beth—a four-hour shift after school and all day on Saturdays, with time in the evenings for homework and seeing John every day and every evening.

She scarfed down the turkey sandwich, drank the pint of velvety brown milk, and joined Miss Edith at the register.

Miss Edith took her by the shoulders. "Child, you don't look like Goldilocks with pink cheeks today. Are you okay?"

"Yes, ma'am. I feel better. A stomach bug, I think, and I haven't felt like eating very much the last few days." After the last long gulp, she threw the empty milk carton in the trash can underneath the counter.

Miss Edith stepped aside and removed her apron. "You gotta eat to keep up your strength, girl. What you need is a big pot of my famous chicken and dumplings."

"Oh no, ma'am. That's too much trouble. But I remember John likes it." Anna Beth reached for her apron under the counter.

Miss Edith shook her head. "Of course he does. Everybody in the neighborhood likes my chicken and dumplings. I think I'll make it anyway. Here it is the last day of March, and the weather's warming up. I don't make this soup in hot weather. When these springtime showers and afternoon thunderstorms start, I know summer will be here almost before those delicate dumplings will be floating in good thick chicken broth and vegetables."

Between practically swallowing a whole turkey sandwich, now churning with chocolate milk in her empty stomach, and listening to Miss Edith talk about floating dumplings, Anna Beth felt the sweat pop out on her brow. She turned and sprinted to the bathroom.

She returned in a few moments, her face still pale, and grabbed her apron.

Miss Edith stepped aside again. "Child, I don't like leaving you here feeling this way. Maybe you need to go back home."

"I'm fine now. I just ate too much on an empty stomach. I'll do my shift, and Alicia's coming over to stay with me tonight."

"You girls having a slumber party on Thursday? Thought slumber parties were reserved for the weekends."

Anna Beth nodded. She had always wanted to have slumber parties like the other girls, but she knew it wasn't safe—not if a friend's mom had conversation with her mom. "No, ma'am. No slumber party. Mom left this morning, going on a trip, and Alicia's coming over to bring my assignments. I didn't feel well enough this morning to go to school. But I'm sure I'll feel better tomorrow."

"Of course you will, because I'm making a pot of goodness, and it's been known to cure everything from a bad cough to a disagreeable colon. You swing by the house on your way home, and I'll have it ready for you. It'll put a hitch in your git-along. Guaranteed." Miss Edith winked at Anna Beth and walked away.

"Yes, ma'am. Thank you. I'll pick up Alicia first. Is eight thirty too late to come by?"

"Are you kidding? It's opening day for major league baseball, and it doesn't matter who's playing, Harry'll be glued to Channel 8 with his eyeballs out on a stem until they turn out the stadium lights. That man loves his baseball. I'll just be crocheting and gently stirring dumplings. Remember to come around to the back door."

"Yes, ma'am. I'll remember."

———•———

Anna Beth clicked the cash-register keys and looked at the clock over the door every few minutes. Her four-hour shift was going by at a snail's pace. Work had never seemed to pass so slowly when John was there. She had constantly searched the aisles for him when she was between customers. They'd steal a knowing glance, and he would find reasons to come to the front to ask her some stupid question. His reasons or questions mattered not to her. Anything John did made her smile.

She really missed him.

Before she left the supermarket after work, she grabbed a loaf of fresh bread, some greens for a salad, a dozen eggs, some fresh strawberries, and a half gallon of ice cream. She knew the cupboard was bare at home. Alicia was coming over, and Anna Beth was hungry. Wanting to eat was a good sign. Maybe the stomach bug had passed.

Lucky for Anna Beth, the old Chevy cranked the first time. John had always given her a ride home, but lately she had been driving her mom's old car to work when she could. Otherwise, she walked.

She picked up Alicia, and the chicken and dumplings from Miss Edith's, and headed home to the small apartment. Once there, she balanced the container and her bag and unlocked the door. She never knew why they bothered to lock it. There was nothing in the apartment of any value or that anyone would want.

She opened the door and reached inside to turn on the light. "Sorry. The place is a mess. Mom left this morning in a hurry, and she was slinging clothes like there's no tomorrow. And I didn't even have time to make the beds before I left for work. At least the kitchen is clean."

"No worries." Alicia plopped her overnight bag on the sofa.

Anna Beth put the soup down on the counter and hung her bag on the back of the chair at the two-chair bistro table. "Yes, but your house is always so clean and neat, and this place looks like the aftermath of a disaster drill."

"Who cares? Just think, in a few months you and John will have your own place. You can make it look like anything you want it to." Alicia followed her into the kitchen.

"Yes, and I cannot wait." She removed the lid from the soup container and inhaled the aroma of homemade chicken and dumplings. "Have you had dinner? Miss Edith made this especially for me, and there's enough to feed your brother's Little League team."

"Sure, I'll have some. Just a small bowl, though. We had

meatloaf and macaroni and cheese for supper."

Anna Beth couldn't remember having homemade meatloaf or a real homemade meal, except when they'd visited her grandma years ago or an occasional meal over at Miss Edith's.

They ate the soup, and while they were enjoying a bowl of ice cream with fresh sliced strawberries, they talked. "Miss Edith has promised to teach me to cook," Anna Beth confided. "She knows her way around the kitchen, and John loves her food."

"Your mom doesn't teach you to cook?" Alicia asked.

"Are you kidding? Look in the cabinet. All you'll see are cans and boxes of instant something. That's Mom's idea of cooking, but Miss Edith really cooks. She uses fresh vegetables, and her casseroles are the best according to John. I want to learn to cook like that—you know, healthy stuff. And I want to sit down to a table that is set with real dishes, and say grace, and pass the food to each other, and help our plates."

Alicia chuckled. "I think you've been watching too many old shows on late-night television."

They finished eating, cleaned the table and the dishes, and headed for the sofa. Anna Beth went over to the shelving where the TV and CD player sat. "Want to listen to Justin Timberlake while we study?"

"Sure. Haven't heard his new album." Alicia sat down at the end of the sofa, opened her bag, and pulled out a notebook. "We'd better go over your assignments. Good news is that there's nothing due tomorrow. You'll whiz by the Algebra II assignment. We can do that together. And Mrs. Madison gave us instructions for a writing assignment that's due on Friday—three descriptive paragraphs of our favorite place and three more paragraphs about why it's our favorite. Guess we could talk about that. I went by and got your assignment from Mr. Hayes. You have some reading for your advanced biology class tomorrow. I cannot imagine taking that class. Save me. I don't really want to know that much about the body."

Anna Beth took the notepaper from Alicia and curled up on the other end of the sofa. "That's my favorite class, and he's my favorite teacher. I think this will give me a head start for nursing school. I'll probably have to take these classes again, but it'll be easier the second time." She looked at Alicia. "I know we need to get started on our homework, but I have something to ask you."

"About what?"

"It's something important to me. And you can say no if you want to. You've been my best friend for a while now, and I would love it if you would be my maid of honor at our wedding. John and I have set the date for October, and Miss Edith is helping me with the plans. Would you be my maid of honor?"

Alicia jumped off the sofa. "Sure. I've never been in a wedding, but I would love to be your maid of honor." Then she froze, practically suspended in midair. "Um, what does a maid of honor do?"

"I've been reading all about it. We don't have time tonight, but maybe you could come over this weekend. I have a stack of wedding magazines in my room. Our wedding will be small and simple. Nothing like those pictures in the magazines, but I want it to be special for John and me to remember. You'll be my only bridesmaid."

"Wow. You're really getting married, and I get to be your maid of honor."

They talked on for a few minutes about dresses and flowers and the wedding cake and pictures and all the things that brides like to talk about. Alicia finally nodded. "Yeah, I'll come back Saturday after your work and spend the weekend. We can talk about it all then. Right now, we'd best start the studying."

Justin Timberlake was crooning "Cry Me a River." Their algebra books and ruled notebooks lay open. With pencils in hand, they chattered about Alicia's crush on Hank between pop-up questions about the wedding and trying to solve quadratic equations. Anna Beth ended up doing most of the solving and explaining why the equations had to be done in a certain sequence.

They were almost finished when Anna Beth's cellphone rang. "Probably Mom checking up on me." She picked up her phone. Ten thirty. The number was unfamiliar. She answered. "Hello."

A male voice. "Uh, yes. Hello. My name is Roy Billingsley. I am trying to reach Anna Beth Nelson."

Anna Beth closed her book and sat up a bit straighter. "This is Anna Beth." She was puzzled, and a sudden worry about her mom shrouded her like a fog in February.

"Miss Nelson, you are listed as the primary contact for John Robert Mitchell."

Anna Beth froze. She had never heard John's full name mentioned in such a tone of voice. "Yes, John is my fiancé." She loved saying that, but she said no more. She couldn't ask.

He was hesitant. "Miss Nelson, are you alone, or is there someone with you?"

"My best friend is here. We're studying." She paused. "Why do you ask?"

"I am afraid I have some bad news. There truly is no easy way to tell you this, but there was an explosion on the rig late this afternoon, and John was one of the casualties. I have no words to tell you how sorry I am, Miss Nelson. Since you were listed as his next of kin, it is my job to notify you."

John. A casualty. One of the casualties. Stunned, she sat in frozen silence.

"Miss Nelson, are you still on the line?"

She tried to speak but words were hard to come. "Yes. Do you mean John is injured?"

"No, ma'am. John was killed in the explosion, along with two others. We know that much. I will call you back with more details tomorrow as we learn them."

"You mean you'll tell me what happened then?"

"Yes, and we can talk about the final arrangements."

Final arrangements? Final. Arrangements. What about wedding plans? She had never made final arrangements. She had no notion of where to start. She was voiceless and in shock.

"Ma'am. I can assure you that we will do everything in our power to bring John's body home for a proper burial. I will call you back tomorrow, if I may." His voice slowed. "And Miss Nelson, again, let me say how very sorry I am that this happened. I would rather tell you anything than what I've just had to relay. May God bring you comfort. I will be in touch. Good night."

The phone slipped from her hand onto the floor. She was suddenly so cold and so still from the inside out.

Alicia closed her book and moved closer to Anna Beth. "You're as white as a sheet, Anna Beth. What was that all about? You look like you've seen a ghost."

In a whispered voice, she replied. "I . . . I think I just did."

"What's that supposed to mean?" Alicia put her arm around Anna Beth's shoulder.

In a whispered voice that cracked with breathlessness, Anna Beth replied, "John is gone."

"Gone? Gone where?"

"I can only hope he's in heaven. John is dead, killed in

an explosion this afternoon. And he took my heart and all our dreams with him."

She fell to her knees on the floor and sobbed.

Chapter Four

April
Jacksonville, Florida

The days since John's memorial service had been a murky, bottomless pit of sorrow and the deepest sadness Anna Beth had ever felt. The world and the people around her moved on like John had never existed, but she was suffocating in the quicksand of grief, with no strength or even desire to pull herself out. Either Miss Edith or Alicia showed up when she felt she could no longer breathe. Somehow, she had just enough strength to reach out for what solace they offered.

She was alone in the world. Except for the two years with John, she had always felt alone. John had shown her a side of life she'd always known existed somewhere, but her hope for that kind of life and love now lay buried in the swirling depths of the Gulf of Mexico. The bodies of the *casualties,* as Mr. Billingsley called them, were never recovered.

Miss Edith and the pastor from her church shouldered the responsibility of planning the memorial service. The church pews were filled with those who knew John or perhaps were just curious. She sat on the pew between her mom and Miss Edith and stared at the eight-by-ten photo on the altar table—John's graduation photo. She thought of how he had matured since then and longed to touch his stubbled beard and to feel his arm around her shoulder.

Images of standing in the doorway of their dream cottage at Christmas, waiting for John to walk through the gate to the front door and take her in his arms, drowned out the hymns and scriptures. She had imagined that scene hundreds of times since he left in January, longing and waiting for his return. The service seemed to carry on in slow motion as she sat surrounded and yet alone—truly alone—in a church full of people. Anna Beth remembered little about the service other than how she felt.

Her mom had come to Jacksonville, fawning over her during the service. Gina stayed two days before returning to Hilton Head, where she and Rodney had taken jobs in a luxury hotel. "We're still living in the camper, but we'll be moving into a nice apartment soon. You just stay here until you graduate, then you can come to Hilton Head. I'll help with the rent here until you finish school. I just know we can get you a good job at this hotel." Void of almost any sensitivity to Anna Beth's loss or her dreams of getting an education, her mom chattered away and moved right on past it. "You'll see. You're going to graduate, and everything will be fine. Just fine."

Fine? How can things be fine when I don't even want to live? I don't care about graduating or nursing school or moving to Hilton Head. It would take energy and light to see the future, and right now, I'm existing in total darkness, and there is no "fine" and no future.

Gina seemed sheepish when she mentioned that she and Rodney were talking about getting married, like she knew it wasn't the time to talk about it and yet could not contain herself.

Anna Beth longed for the kind of bubble her mother lived in, a bubble that shielded her from reality and protected her from the desperation that grew from deep places.

It had been five days since the funeral service. Her mom had returned to Hilton Head three days ago. Alicia was back in school, and Miss Edith was at the supermarket. They were all moving on and telling her that she had to do the same.

At three o'clock in the afternoon, still in her worn night shirt, Anna Beth shuffled from her bed to the kitchen. She had to eat. She had been living alone the last couple of months. She had known when her mother left with Rodney in February that she wasn't coming back. The apartment was emptier now than ever, except for Miss Edith's casserole and pot of soup.

Anna Beth floundered into the kitchen. Before she opened the refrigerator, she glanced at the wall. There it was—the calendar, hanging next to the kitchen window. The calendar with postcard-like pictures of Florida beaches, the one given out every Christmas at the supermarket. She walked over and lifted each page slowly to see all the dates she had circled or had doodled on: a graduation cap on the Thursday in May when John would come home for her graduation; a stethoscope on the June Monday she would start nursing school; a smiley face on the July Saturday of John's week-long visit; two red hearts on the late September day of his return from the oil rig; two doves on her October wedding date; and the sketch of a cottage with a Christmas tree in the window on December 25, the day that she dreamed of more than her wedding day.

She snatched the calendar from the bare nail on the kitchen wall, ripped into as many pieces as she could, and threw it in the trash. Sadness seized her and would not let go. In its grip, she cried hard. There was no one there to hear her. Banging her fists on the counter, she cried for as long as she had strength to stand.

She was tired, so tired. Exhausted from crying. Drained of any life. Weary of the fatigue and the constant uneasiness that had taken up residence in her stomach in the past few weeks. She hadn't eaten all day. Miss Edith would call her tonight and ask if she had. Anna Beth opened the refrigerator and pulled out the casserole Miss Edith had left—chicken, rice, and broccoli, a full meal in one bowl. She spooned out a hefty helping and went for the microwave.

She had just finished eating and putting her bowl in the dishwasher when there was a ring at the door. She looked at the clock.

Too early for Alicia.

She walked to the door and looked through the peep hole. A delivery man holding a box. Fearing her appearance would alarm him, she opened the door slightly with the chain lock still in place and spoke to him. "Yes? I cannot open the door now. May I help you?"

"Ma'am, I have a delivery of three boxes for Miss Anna Beth Nelson."

Boxes? She had not placed an order. "Are you certain they're for me?"

"If you're Anna Beth Nelson, they are."

"Could you please just leave them on the stoop?"

He put the box down. "Ma'am, I can do that, but these boxes do require a signature. Could you sign here while I get the other two?"

She opened the door and took the clipboard from him

and signed on the line he designated. He returned with two larger boxes on a hand truck. "Ma'am, these are large, but they're not heavy. I'll be happy to set them inside the door if you'd like."

She handed him the clipboard. "That's a kind offer. But no, thank you. I can get them." She waited until the driver was back in the truck, went out on the stoop, and pulled the boxes inside. She pushed the coffee table aside and lugged them to the sofa. She didn't have the strength to stand and open them.

The return address was the name of the company that had hired John to work on the oil rig. She remembered Mr. Billingsley saying they'd be shipping John's personal effects to her.

Looking at the boxes, she was transported back to her grandma's house when her mom and her aunt were going through her grandma's things after her funeral. She'd been only nine, but she remembered how they'd tossed her grandma's clothes into a bag and swiped everything from her dresser into a garbage can. They showed no emotion, no feeling, just a desire to get it over with. The only things they fussed over were the box of her grandma's handmade Christmas ornaments and a collection of spoons. Her mom had gotten the tub of Christmas decorations. Still in the back end of Anna Beth's closet, they were the only thing to prove she had a family.

Anna Beth would not treat John's belongings with such disrespect. She went to the kitchen for scissors and returned to open the boxes. She removed the tape from each box with the same care she would have used to remove the bandages from John's wounds.

All that was left of John lay in these three boxes and in the memories she hoarded in her heart.

She opened them to find mostly his clothes. Work shirts

with his name embroidered. T-shirts—the ones he wore on the beach. Photos of Anna Beth. Printed emails they had written to each. His wallet with their photo from the beach festival. His driver's license. A bottle of aftershave. His airline ticket for her graduation. Sparse belongings, but evidence that he had loved her and was longing to return to her.

Her tears stained the boxes as she carefully repacked them, saving everything and leaving out a few of his T-shirts and the photos that she would take to her room later. She removed her night shirt, slipped her favorite of John's shirts over her head, and lay back, resting her head on the pillow. His other shirts she held over her face. They smelled of him.

She cried until her lower abdomen began to cramp. Changing positions, she rolled to her side and pulled her knees up tight. She rubbed her belly, and her thoughts became unsettled, much like the feeling in the pit of her stomach.

—•—

A few days later on Sunday afternoon

With graduation barely a month away, Anna Beth was planning to return to school on Monday. Her teachers had been understanding and encouraging during her two-week absence. Alicia had been her liaison to bring her assignments and to return her work to her teachers during her absence. She simply had not been able to keep up with all her assignments, but her grades were not in jeopardy. Graduating in the top five percent of her class was still a given.

She had one task she had put off—John's storage unit. When Miss Edith called again and asked about going on Sunday afternoon, she finally agreed.

She picked up Miss Edith, and they drove over to the industrial area to find the unit where John had stored his furniture and other possessions after he moved from his apartment. He had left the key with Mr. Harry, Miss Edith's husband, after he helped John clear out his apartment and move things into storage.

They located the unit, and Anna Beth unlocked the door. They spent a few minutes looking around. Furniture, a mattress, several boxes stacked on top of each other, a bicycle. Most likely clothes, linens, and kitchen stuff in the boxes, according to Miss Edith.

"Look, Anna Beth, John would want you to have everything in here. He didn't have any other family. Parents dead, and no siblings. I don't know about aunts or uncles. He never mentioned them. Nobody but friends showed up for his funeral. So, I think you should just take whatever you want, and you can sell the rest or give it away. You do remember John listed you as his next of kin on his paperwork, and that's why Mr. Billingsley sent you the boxes of John's personal belongings from the oil rig, and he'll be sending the money they were holding in John's account. So, who's going to fuss about John's other belongings? No one. Take what you'd like."

Anna Beth was overwhelmed. She looked around the small unit—just more of John that she wasn't ready to let go of. "Okay, Miss Edith. I've seen what's here. I think I'll keep the unit for now until I can decide what to do with these things. I don't think my mom is ever coming back to Jacksonville, and I haven't had my thoughts together enough to know what I will do after graduation."

"What do you mean you don't know?" She felt Miss

Edith's grip on her arm as she locked the door on the storage unit. "You don't need to get your thoughts together for that. You'll do what you planned to do and what John would want you to do. You'll walk that stage in a few weeks, take that diploma proudly. With what you've saved and the money John left, you should have a good start to nursing school in June."

"Maybe I will." Miss Edith did not know what had been keeping Anna Beth awake for the last couple of nights. "But for sure, I will be back in school in the morning and back to work tomorrow afternoon. Thank you for coming here with me today. I'll begin to think about what to do with John's things, and if there's anything you want, please take it. John loved you and Mr. Harry, and he'd want you to have something too. But for now, I'd best get you back home, and I need to pick up Alicia. She's staying the night and going to school with me in the morning."

Anna Beth locked the storage unit. She was quiet on the drive to Miss Edith's house. But Alicia was all smiles when Anna Beth picked her up. "Hey, you want to go to the beach and get a hot dog before we go back to your place? Maybe we could take long walk or a jog. No homework. We should celebrate."

"I don't think so. I've had it for the day. I just want to go back to the apartment." As they made the drive, she told Alicia about what was in the storage unit.

Once inside, Anna Beth took Alicia's arm and practically pulled her toward the sofa. "You don't know how glad I am you're staying over tonight. I can't do this by myself. There's something I haven't told you because I'm not sure I can even say it out loud."

"Ouch. You're really squeezing my arm. So, what is it? We tell each other everything. Tell me."

"Sit down first." They sat on the sofa side by side. Anna

Beth scratched the palms of her hands, a nervous habit, and then took a deep breath. "There's no easy way to say this, so I'll just say it outright. I think I'm pregnant."

No words. Only Alicia's face responded—jaw dropped, eyes wide, nostrils flared.

"I've been reading about how to know if you're pregnant, and I really think I am. I have all the signs." Anna Beth reached into her tote bag. "So, I bought this." She pulled out a home pregnancy test. "But I couldn't do this alone. That's why I'm glad you're here."

Alicia fumbled for words. "You think you're pregnant?" She looked away. "Did you tell John, before, I mean . . .?"

"No. I didn't really think about it until the last couple of days. I've told no one. It's the first time I've said it out loud. I can't tell my mom. She's not here, and I'm sort of glad. And this isn't really something I want to talk to Miss Edith about yet, not until I know for sure. But you're my friend, and I knew I could count on you." She handed Alicia the box. "Do you know anything about these?"

Again, Alicia's faced responded in surprise. "Ah . . . no. Not much. I've never really seen one. I know other girls who have used them. But it can't be that difficult. I mean it *is* a home pregnancy test."

"I've read the directions, and you're right, it's not that complicated. I just couldn't do it alone. Read them and see what you think."

They read the directions together. Alicia nodded. "Yeah, you can do this. It's kind of simple. No way to mess up."

Anna Beth took a deep breath. "Okay, will you come with me? You can just stand outside the bathroom door."

"Sure." Alicia followed her down the hallway and leaned against the wall while Anna Beth went inside and closed the bathroom door.

Five minutes later, Anna Beth, holding the test stick in

her hand, opened the door. "Here, look. What do you think?"

Alicia took the test stick, looked closely, and compared it to the picture on the package directions. She extended the paper to Anna Beth and said slowly and deliberately, "According to the directions, I think you're pregnant."

Anna Beth gasped, turned to throw the test stick into the bathroom trash can, and walked down the hall to her bedroom with Alicia following. She sat on the edge of her bed and gently rubbed her belly. "I bought another test kit in case, but I don't think I need to do it again. It's positive. Real positive."

She could sense Alicia's hesitancy in her next question. "Do you know how pregnant? I mean how many weeks?"

"Yes, we . . . made love only once, and that was the night before he left in late January, the night we got engaged. He was always so respectful." She paused. "So, I must be close to twelve weeks. Now, I know why I've not been feeling so well."

Alicia asked, "How *do* you feel? I mean, I know you've been under the weather, but how do you feel about being pregnant? Are you going to have the baby?"

Anna Beth quickly turned a resolute face toward Alicia. "I will forget you asked me that question. Yes. I am having this baby."

Alicia retorted, "I was just thinking that John is gone, and I do know a couple of girls who decided they didn't want to be young mothers. They didn't want their babies. So . . ."

"Well, I'm not one of those girls. This is John's baby, and it's all I have left of him. I could not . . . No, I could never not have this baby."

Alicia responded with quiet calm. "Maybe you should give yourself a little time to think about it. A baby could really complicate your life, Anna Beth."

Anna Beth felt the tightness in her whole abdomen. "Mr. Billingsley called John a *casualty*, and now you're calling this baby a *complication*. John was a person, the man I loved. He had a name, and so will our baby, and I will love this baby with all that is in me."

"Okay. I get it. So, since you've decided to keep it, what are you going to do?"

Anna Beth hung her head and stared at the floor. For just a moment, she allowed herself to cry and then lifted her head to answer. "I don't know, but I do know three things right now. I will graduate. I will have this baby. And I will love it and try to be the best mother I can be. I've had good lessons in how to be a lousy one." She paused. "I'll figure it out as I go. Right now, I don't know how I'll make it, but I'll have to, won't I?"

Chapter Five

Late May
Bar Haven

"Happy Monday morning, boys! On the countdown. Just three more days of school and kindergarten, then we have the whole summer." Jillian brought bowls of oatmeal with fresh blueberries and strawberries to Reese and Riley at the table, and she put a bowl of scrambled eggs between them, knowing Reese would gladly let Riley have them all. "Your cinnamon raisin toast is almost done."

Riley could not resist. He picked up a whole plump strawberry with his fingers and put it in his mouth. Then, in garbled speech, he said, "I want peanut butter on my toast, Mama."

Jillian turned from the oven to look at her young son. "Seems you're forgetting something, Riley."

Riley bowed his head, closed his eyes, and folded his hands under his chin, still chewing the sweet berry.

"That's better, she said." A moment later she served

their toast and sat down with her cup of coffee and her calendar. "And you know what would even be better is if you didn't forget next time."

"But Mama, I'm so hungry, and that strawberry just looked so good."

"Um-huh, that same story got the whole human race into a lot of trouble."

"What's a human race, Mama?" Riley asked.

"Well, first let's thank God together for the strawberries and everything else you're about to eat, and then maybe your older brother will explain it to you." She looked at Reese, whose eyes were rolling, curious to hear how he would address the question.

Spoons entered the warm oatmeal while the *n* was still resonating on Jillian's *amen*. Riley picked up a blueberry that had fallen off his spoon and had almost rolled off the table and put it in his mouth. "What's a human race, Reese?"

"The human race is all human beings, all the people who have ever lived on planet Earth since the beginning of time."

Jillian looked at Riley's puzzled expression but decided not to intervene.

"Yeah, but what kinda race? We do races in kindergarten all the time, and I win a lot. Me and Frankie won a three-legged race yesterday."

"It's not that kind of race, Riley. It's just an expression."

Still with food in his mouth, Riley continued, "Mama said something got 'em in trouble. Did somebody cheat on the race?"

"No. It's not a race for competing. Some words can mean more than one thing—like *season* can mean spring or summer or like Mama seasoned your eggs this morning with salt and pepper. Just think of the human race as all human beings. We're not fish or birds. We're human beings and the human race."

Riley's curiosity and persistence put a smile on his mother's face. "That's all mixed up. And who got into trouble?"

Jillian could tell Reese's patience was waning with his brother's never-ending curiosity.

"It was Eve, the very first woman. God made Adam and Eve and let them live in the Garden of Eden, and God told them not to pick fruit and eat it from this one tree in the garden. Kinda like I tell you to leave things, especially my drawings, alone and ask me before you take them. But a snake showed up in the garden and told Eve to do it. She listened to the snake instead of God. She picked the fruit, ate it, and gave it to Adam to eat too. And there's been trouble ever since."

"You mean snakes talk? And did she eat a strawberry?"

Riley's eyes grew wide with wonder, and Jillian thought it time to step in. "Riley, there are some things you will understand a little better when you're older, like your brother." She had long ago learned the art of deflection when Reese was just a tot. "Okay, so today your dad left early for St. Simons. He has an audit there, but he'll be back in time to take you to your T-ball game this afternoon, Riley. Some of the ladies from church are coming over to our house for a meeting this afternoon. Reese, do you mind walking home from school? I checked the weather, and it's not supposed to rain."

"No, ma'am. Since all the ladies will be here, could I walk over to the beach and take my sketch pad? It would be closer to walk from school."

"That would be just fine unless you need to study for some final exams. I trust you to know what you should do." She stood from the table and closed her calendar. "You might put an apple and a granola bar in your backpack. I know you, and you'll be hungry. Just be home by five."

Reese stood and took his empty plate and bowl to the sink. "If the weather's nice, I may take my watercolors too."

"Okay, boys, five minutes to brush your teeth and be downstairs. Your lunch boxes are ready, and I'll take you to school. Then I'm spending the morning in the carriage-house apartment doing the spring cleaning and going through some more of Gramps' boxes."

———•———

Holding on to her cleaning caddy, Jillian climbed the steps and unlocked the carriage apartment. She wedged the door stop under the front door, opened the French doors to the back-porch balcony, and raised all the windows. The spring breezes would flow right through and bring the scent of the jasmine mixed with the salt air.

She did the normal cleaning in less than an hour and looked around the apartment, admiring her work and making a mental list of things she wanted to do to refresh and update the place. Gramps had turned over the big house to Jillian and Stuart and had moved into the carriage apartment just a few months after his wife died. He had built the Victorian-style carriage house—a garage below and living quarters above. Continuing to live in the home of his birth, even if it was in the apartment, brought comfort to him in his last years. He told Jillian he felt like one of the mourning doves perched in the moss-laden oak tree. Front windows gave him a bird's-eye view of the main house and the boys outside playing, and the balcony out back showcased the sunrise over the Atlantic.

The carriage house was at least thirty yards from the main house and had its own entrance and stairs that led from the driveway. The kitchen was small but quite functional, and the living area was spacious with plenty of natural light. It seemed a shame to leave this two-bedroom, two-bath apartment vacant when it could be earning a few hundred dollars a month instead of collecting dust. Renting the apartment could provide a bit of extra income. After all, it took money to keep up this sprawling place, and they had two sons who would need college educations. She thought of approaching Stuart with the idea of renting it. Jillian was blessed not to have to worry about finances and paying bills. Stuart did all of that.

A few pieces of new furniture that had not already lived through at least four decades with Gramps, new curtains, a coat of fresh paint, something on the walls beside framed and faded prints of sailing vessels, and this place could be cozy and comfortable for someone. Maybe a young couple just starting out. Or maybe an older couple looking for a smaller place. Her morning thoughts motivated her to at least speak with Stuart about the possibility.

Jillian walked to the bedroom and opened the double louvered closet doors to three stacks of boxes. Gramps' clothes had already been given away after Stuart had saved a few of his ties and cuff links for himself and the boys. Now it was down to the boxes that Stuart's mother had packed away years ago. Gramps had probably never opened them. But it was time.

She was surprised to find a few boxes of what seemed to be Stuart's mother's clothes. But upon closer scrutiny, she began to find paper strips safety-pinned to the articles. She strained to make out the faded writing describing the articles and whose they were. Granny O'Hara, affectionately called Granny O by her grandchildren, had packed away some of her mother's and grandmother's clothing. Suddenly these dusty, disintegrating cardboard boxes had turned into treasure troves of lovely vintage clothing from three generations ago. Silk scarves, lovely shawls, lace gloves, handsewn aprons, and Granny O's wedding dress—pieces of clothing that connected this family's stories over three generations and two continents. These pieces, so loved by Granny O, deserved better than a cardboard box. But what?

Within half an hour, five of the boxes were empty and the queen-sized bed was covered with carefully folded articles that told family stories.

Now curious about other treasures, she continued to open boxes. A smaller box contained letters written by Gramps' seafaring father, whose dream it had been to build this house for his family. Jillian took the box, sat in the wooden rocker next to the window, and pulled the letters out one by one, always careful with the brittle paper that was nearly a century old.

Captain O'Hara wrote often of his adventures and of his longing for home—the home he'd built for his wife and son near the sea he loved. The letters were postmarked from faraway places. She hoped that Gramps had read the letters written by his parents to each other. When he had spoken of his father, it was mostly of his father's absence, but these letters told of his father's love for him and for his mother.

Jillian found herself sitting in the wooden rocker next to the window for the next hour, reading about ports of call, exotic birds, storms at sea, and the different colors of sunrises and sunsets off the coast of South America. The captain had written about the strange blue-footed boobies and determined frigate birds. His wife replied with tales of how well their son was doing in school, about newcomers to the community, and the mourning doves and marsh wrens that serenaded them daily.

Then came the box of architectural drawings of the house and carriage house. These drawings were covered with notes scribbled in pencil by Gramps, his plans for the next addition to the house. Presently, she and her family lived in what had once been a dream and a drawing.

More treasures that shouldn't be packed away but remain visible so that Reese and Riley could know about their heritage. She hoped someday one of them would want the house, and she and Stuart could move into the carriage house.

The last three boxes were Christmas ornaments. As Jillian unwrapped them, she realized the ornaments would have been on the Christmas tree when Gramps was a child. His mother had made hand-painted ornaments for his first Christmas and the next eighteen Christmases until Gramps had married. Some were glass. Some were wooden, but all were dated. Such detail in everything from the manger scene to Baby Jesus cuddled in His mother's arms to a pair of mourning doves on the limb of an oak tree.

Perhaps Reese's gift for painting was an inherited one. She imagined that each ornament had been something special to Gramps and his mother. In his father's absence, they had been so close.

She rewrapped each one carefully and returned them to their boxes, except the one with the mourning doves. The pair of doves perched together on a limb was painted on a piece of driftwood that had been sanded smooth. The brush strokes and detail were amazing, and she wondered if the tree in the painting was of the huge old oak out back shading the carriage house, now at least seventy years older.

She would ask Stuart about that later and purchase proper storage bins for all the ornaments to preserve them. In her imagination, she saw them on the family tree in the gathering room next to the fireplace. These ornaments would decorate that tree this Christmas, probably their first Christmas in over fifty years, and she would add the ones she had made for Reese and Riley. She only wished Gramps was here to see it and tell the stories.

With the windows open, Jillian could hear the bells from the belltower in town. It was noon. She had not intended to spend the entire morning unpacking boxes. She would look forward to returning to her treasure hunting tomorrow, but for now she needed to get back to the house for a bite of lunch, a shower, and preparation before Rosemary and the other ladies arrived. She closed the windows, brushed the dust from her blouse and shorts, and took the one ornament with her. Unlike her usual self, she left the folded vintage clothing scattered in stacks across the bed with opened boxes dotting the floor and closed the bedroom door.

Shutting the rest of the windows and the French doors, she locked the door to the apartment and held tightly to the ornament as she walked back to the house. She wondered what Reese would think when he saw it.

———•———

Four o'clock. Stuart had picked up Riley and was probably already at the ballfield. Jillian was ready and looking forward to her visitors. She had prepared the table, showered, put on her new mint-green cotton dress, and brushed her auburn curls into place where they just touched her shoulders. A contented housewife and mother, she stayed busy every day taking care of her family and participating in church and community activities.

Stuart had been one of the first people she met as a college freshman at the University of North Carolina. Soon after they met, they'd become inseparable. She had grown up as a city girl in Asheville, but when Stuart proposed just before their college graduation, she excitedly accepted.

Stuart had brought her to Bar Haven several times during their college years. The town, which was more like a village, lured her, and she imagined a beautiful life as Stuart's wife. With fond memories of family vacations on North Carolina's Outer Banks, she was at home in the marshlands of the Georgia coast.

Bar Haven's small-town life was just that: small-town life. Like the O'Haras, many families had lived here for generations in homes built by their ancestors in this peaceful seaside community where everyone counted, even the ornery ones. They took care of each other, even the ornery ones. When the storms came, they helped each other batten down the hatches, even the ones belonging to the ornery ones. When someone was down on his luck, townsfolk pitched in. No fanfare. Nothing expected in return. It was just what the good folks in Bar Haven did.

Bar Haven was known for its Christmas celebrations. Multicolored Christmas lights that lit up the town could be seen in the distance up and down the coastline. People drove for miles to hear the Christmas music at the local church, and it overflowed with visitors on Christmas Eve. There was only one church in the village. One street through town, and the church sat at the end of that street.

When Rosemary Franklin, the pastor's wife, came up with the idea of the live nativity scene for the Sunday evening before Christmas, all the church ladies got involved. That meant their husbands and children would get involved too.

This afternoon's meeting was just to check in to see where the ladies were in their preparations and assignments. It could have easily been done with a few phone calls, but they enjoyed getting together, especially if Jillian was the host. Hers was always a tea party.

Her table was set with her grandmother's china and

linen tea napkins, fresh flowers from the garden, crustless finger sandwiches made with pimiento cheese or cream cheese and fresh cucumbers, fresh-baked lemon cookies, and scones with Jillian's homemade strawberry preserves and her version of clotted cream. And then there was the tea, a fine black tea, the kind served at Harrod's in London, and even a bergamot tea for those who liked it. It was tea fit for a queen.

As far as Jillian was concerned, the pastor's wife was their queen. Rosemary was fast approaching seventy. She and her husband had served this community with faithfulness and creativity for the last four decades. Rosemary had done everything from playing the organ to coaching their Little League baseball team when their sons were small. She was a fine seamstress and just as good with a hammer and nails. She had delivered more food baskets than the Easter Bunny. She had held the hands of the dying and the bereaved. She had even delivered a baby once, not because she was a medic but because she was there when needed.

Rosemary, her short curls a dull silver, was a bit rotund now, and her photo could appear next to the word *granny* in the dictionary, but she was no less energetic than she'd been thirty years ago. So, when she'd suggested a live nativity scene, the church members had promised to make that happen. Their first job had been to figure out how to make it appear live without real animals.

The ladies gathered and took their customary seats at Jillian's spacious dining table. The lace curtains floated on the afternoon breeze coming through the large windows. The ladies enjoyed the treats and catching up, but when Rosemary decided to start the meeting, it was started.

"First of all, ladies, I think we should thank Jillian for such a lovely spread this afternoon. We have been treated like royalty." All the ladies looked Jillian's way and clapped daintily. "Jillian, of your many gifts, I do believe your gift of hospitality tops the list." The ladies clapped again.

Jillian felt her face flush and accepted their attention with a quiet thank you and a lowered head.

Rosemary continued. "Now on to the business. I know it's only May, and Christmas is several months away, but we need to be ready. And besides, doing it this way, we're just celebrating Christmas all year long. This live nativity is not just for visitors at Christmas. It's to keep Christmas in our hearts all through the year." She turned to Linda. "How are you coming with the costumes?"

Linda reported her committee had purchased patterns, designed all the costumes, and they were to order the fabric next week. She had located a church in Savannah that had offered to let her borrow three fancy crowns for the Wise Men from their collection of pageant costumes.

"Well, that's mighty fine for this year. You just get those costumes made, and next year, we'll make our own crowns and start our own costume department."

Next came Suellen, who reported that her husband had drawn the plans for the crèche itself and had enlisted the help of a couple of the other men to assist in its construction. It would be erected from wood and covered with palmetto branches on site a few days before the event. The manger would sit on seagrass mixed with hay.

Rosemary responded happily. "Sounds like progress to me. Since camels and sheep are hard to come by around here, and they would require feeding and cleaning up after, aren't we fortunate to have Buck and Reese helping us out? Jillian, can you give us an update."

"Yes, ma'am. Reese spent his spring break with Mr. Buckingham getting those life-sized animals cut out of plywood. The camel is authentic and even has two humps. Now I'm happy to say they're in storage waiting to be painted. Reese is painting them as he has time. He'll have all summer to finish this project."

Rosemary added, "It's a fine young man who'll spend his spring break and summer painting a camel, a donkey, and some sheep."

Jillian nodded. "Forgive me for sounding like a proud mother, but I've seen one of the sheep, and Reese is doing an outstanding job. I wish I had his talent."

Rosemary chuckled. "No need to apologize for being a proud mother. The world would be a better place if there were more mothers who were proud of their children, and told them so, and told everybody else too." Rosemary paused. "Well, ladies, I'm lining up the music and I'll give you more information about that at our next meeting. I've been praying and waiting to hear that one of our young ladies is pregnant so that we'll have a real baby in the manger. Let me know the minute you hear of one, and I'll be on her front doorsteps with a basket of baby goodies before she has time to sing a lullaby."

She grinned and winked. "I suppose we had better adjourn and get home before suppertime. I don't think any of us have husbands who know their way around the kitchen and will have our evening meals on the table when we get home."

They all laughed and nodded in agreement, stood from their chairs, and followed Rosemary to the front door. Jillian stood on the porch with a happy heart, watching the ladies leave two by two down the pebbled walkway to the gate, hearing their laughter, and knowing her guys would be home in about an hour. She watched as Rosemary stopped to smell the sweet shrub before she unlatched the wooden gate and stood as the ladies filed out before closing the gate, returning the latch, and waving. Jillian waved back and closed the door, satisfied with her beautiful day. But she had other things on her mind.

As was their custom at their evening meal, the O'Haras talked about their day and listened to each other—really listened—even as they passed the pork-chop platter, the bowl of peas and carrots, the rice and gravy, and the pear salad. Their conversation continued until the meal was finished and dessert had been served. This was how the O'Haras did dinner and put the period at the end of each day.

Stuart had found his drive to and from St. Simons relaxing but was glad to have finished the audit. Riley had lost his T-ball game but declared that he had played well. Jillian knew Riley's understanding of "playing well" meant his bat had actually made contact with the ball. It mattered not to him what happened after that. He had done his part. Reese showed them the watercolor seascape he had painted that afternoon.

Jillian was always amazed at his talent and knew that her oldest son saw the world differently from most folks. "Why, Reese, that is beautiful. And I think I have just the spot for it. Leave this one with me unless you'd like to go with me to choose a frame."

"It's not really that good, Mama. You don't have to frame it."

She beamed at his modesty. "I'd like to frame it, and I truly do have just the spot for it." She was remembering a place next to the French doors in the carriage apartment. "I didn't know this evening would turn into a show-and-tell, but I have something to show too." She stood and retrieved the hand-painted Christmas ornament. "I was going through the last of the boxes in Gramps' apartment this morning. I was like one of those divers who explore sunken ships to find treasure chests. And I did find some treasures. I found clothes that belonged to your grandmother's grandmother. That means she would be your great-great-grandmother. I found a box of letters that Gramps' parents wrote to each other when he was sailing the seas. And then I opened a box to find hand-painted Christmas ornaments that Gramps' mother had made for him."

She held up the rectangular piece of wood dangling from a ribbon. "This was my favorite. Look, Reese, your great-grandmother was quite an artist. She painted these two mourning doves, and I think this is the oak tree out back." She turned the ornament so that Stuart could see. "What do you think?"

Stuart agreed. Reese sat quietly staring at the small painting.

"You remember how Gramps loved listening to the mourning doves?" Jillian asked. "And they still roost in the oak tree seventy years later. I heard them this morning."

Riley looked puzzled. "Those are some old birds if they're still flying around."

They all laughed.

"No, Riley. They're not the same birds, but the doves still like to come here to roost in that tree. Maybe the doves we hear are descendants of the doves your great-grandmother painted, just like we're descendants of the ones who built this house." Jillian turned to her husband. "I've been thinking, Stuart. I'd really like to fix up the apartment and call it Dove's Landing. We could rent it out to an older couple or a young couple just starting out. That way, it could be useful. I wouldn't have to clean it, and it would bring in some income. What do you think?"

Stuart smiled. "Dove's Landing, you say? Maybe we should give that some thought."

Jillian didn't miss the wink Stuart gave Reese nor the sheepish grin Reese returned.

Chapter Six

———◆———

Late May
Jacksonville, Florida

Anna Beth eyed the clock. One twenty. She looked at the flowers and the table set for the lunch she had prepared for her mom's arrival. Her mom was supposed to be here at eleven, but Gina was late as usual. At least she had called this time. Anna Beth could only hope she would arrive in time for graduation. Otherwise, there would be no family to watch her walk the stage. Miss Edith was filling in for Anna Beth's shift at the supermarket, so she would not be there. Only her friend Alicia, who was also graduating, would be there for her.

Rodney and Gina's new life in Hilton Head had consumed Gina, and she had expressed about as much interest in Anna Beth lately as she did in reporting her waitressing tips on her income tax returns. She usually called once a week to tell Anna Beth how hard she was working and how Rodney was treating her, occasionally asking if Anna Beth had a new boyfriend or if she needed money for the rent. There had been no mention of Anna Beth's plans to go to nursing school. Wanting it to be a surprise, Anna Beth had not told her that she would be graduating near the top of her class and that she would be receiving an honors award in science. She hoped that would soften the blow coming later.

Anna Beth breathed easier knowing that Rodney was not coming. Her graduation honors were not all that would be a surprise to her mom, and she was relieved Rodney would not be present for the conversation after her big announcement.

Anna Beth finished pressing her graduation gown and laid it across the bed. Graduation exercises would begin at three o'clock, and she had to be there at two for roll call and for lining up with just over four hundred other graduates. She thought of the party Alicia's parents were hosting to celebrate their daughter's graduation. Her grandparents, aunts, uncles, cousins, and a few friends were all coming over for a backyard barbecue. Alicia had invited Anna Beth, but Anna Beth had declined, explaining that she needed to have time with her mom. Alicia was the only one who knew why.

How Anna Beth wished John was here. He would have made sure there was at least a small celebration of her accomplishments, and he would have assured her mom that he would take care of Anna Beth and their baby. She still had the airline ticket he had purchased, and her eyes filled with tears to think he wouldn't be here for graduation or for the wedding they were planning or for anything else ever. It was still surreal to her that she would never see him again on this side of heaven and that he would never know she had a child. If she had only known and could have told him, then she would have truly felt it was their child. As of late, she only thought of the baby as hers, and hers alone.

She slipped on her mom's navy broomstick skirt and white overblouse, went to her dresser, brushed her blond curls, and tried on her graduation cap. She looked at the framed picture of her and John and turned to look at the profile of her body in the mirror. Gently rubbing the slight bulge in her belly, she glanced at the picture on the dresser again, wondering if her baby would be blond like her or have dark hair like John.

Anna Beth had been experiencing the normal pregnancy changes in her body. There had been no one except Alicia to talk to about those changes, and she was anxious to ask her mom about her experience. What Anna Beth knew she had learned in her biology class and in online searches. No doctor's visit yet. Just over-the-counter prenatal vitamins she had read about. Only able to handle and juggle so much alone, she had deliberately postponed the doctor visit and decisions about her future until after graduation. Mr. Billingsley had sent her a check for John's holdings. With that money in the bank, she hoped to be able to afford a doctor. There was no way to know how her mom would react, but no matter her reaction, Anna Beth would not tell her about the money she had saved or the money coming from John's company.

She adjusted the overblouse and was grateful that her pregnancy was unnoticeable even with her slight frame. But she knew she was into her second trimester now, and her body would be undergoing quite noticeable changes from here on out. Only she and Alicia knew that she would walk the stage as an unmarried pregnant girl. But in her heart, she was married. She still proudly wore the engagement ring to fulfill her promise to John that she would never remove it from her finger.

Her graduation gown draped over her arm and with cap in hand, she left the apartment feeling not like an excited graduate but more like a neglected child, a bereaved widow, and a hopeless mother-to-be. Graduation would change little except she would have a high-school diploma in her hand. Her heart and mind would still churn with unanswered questions.

———·———

After the tossing of the caps, a couple of hugs from her classmates, and pats on the back from her science and English teachers, Anna Beth heard her mother's voice. Gina approached hurriedly with open arms in her smarmy, fawning way, kissing Anna Beth's cheeks, stroking her hair, and spouting syrupy words that turned Anna Beth's already queasy stomach.

"Oh, my smart, intelligent girl." Gina turned to all around and spewed some more. "Would you look at this beautiful girl? Graduating at the top of her class with honors in science. She is her mother's daughter." She turned to kiss Anna Beth's cheeks again.

"Stop it, Mom," Anna Beth said quietly. "I need to turn in my cap and gown, and I want to say goodbye to Alicia."

"Okay, Sugar Pie. I'll follow you."

Anna Beth returned her cap and gown, gave Alicia a hug, and solemnly took her mother's hand and led her out of the crowd. Smothering kisses and flattery for the sake of others could not erase months or maybe a lifetime of neglect. Gina's parenting was like a knock-off perfume—similar but counterfeit, sweet-smelling for only a short time, and made of elements harmful to humans.

In stilettos, Gina struggled to keep up with Anna Beth. "Oh, Sugar Pie, I'm so very proud of you. Why didn't you tell me about this, the honors and all?"

Anna Beth was determined not to start a scene in the

parking lot by telling her mom it was because she never seemed interested. Instead, she said, "I just wanted it to be a nice surprise for you, Mom. Where's your car?"

"Oh, the parking lot was full when I got here. It's way over on the backside of the lot. Maybe you could drive me over there. And then we'll go for a nice early dinner to celebrate. What's your favorite place?"

Anna Beth was not about to spoil the memory of her favorite restaurant with a dinner with her mom. Her favorite place belonged only to her and John. "Let's just go back to the apartment. I'm tired, and I'd really like to go home. I had prepared an extra-special lunch for you. It's in the fridge, and we can eat that. Your favorite. Lobster salad. Hop in, and I'll take you to your car."

Gina settled into the passenger seat. "But I'm all dressed up, and you are, too, and I'd like to take you out. You can eat that stuff you made tomorrow when I'm not here."

"But aren't you staying the night?"

"No, Sugar Pie, I'm driving back tonight. It's only a three-hour drive, and I told Rodney I'd be home by eleven. But you and I have plenty of time to go out to eat."

Anna Beth looked at her watch. Almost five thirty. A quick calculation—her mom would need to leave by eight o'clock. That meant only a couple of hours to talk. "No, Mom, it's my day to celebrate, and I want to go home."

Gina badgered. "But you look so nice, and I haven't done anything for your graduation. At least let me do this."

Anna Beth turned the key in the ignition. "No, Mom. I want to go home." Then with a hint of snarkiness, she asked, "You still remember how to get there, don't you?" She didn't bother to look her mom's way.

"Well, didn't my little Sugar Pie turn into a sour puss with one door slam? I don't like your attitude. What's making you so mean?"

Anna Beth drove through the parking lot to her mom's car in silence.

Maybe it's because Alicia's parents are throwing her a big party to celebrate with her whole family, and I have to make my own party. Maybe it's because I spent my week's grocery money on lobster, salad fixings, a loaf of artisan bread, and a real cake from the bakery, decorated for my graduation. And you didn't even show up. Or maybe because you haven't shown up in so long I can't remember. Or maybe it's because I'm pregnant, alone, and frightened out of my wits.

But Anna Beth muzzled herself, knowing if she started talking, it would be like a break in the Rodman Dam. She wouldn't be able to stop, and the damage could be cataclysmic. As angry as she could be with her mom, she understood why she was the kind of mother she was. Gina parented just like she'd been parented, but Anna Beth was determined to break that cycle. That kind of absentee parenting would stop with her.

"I don't mean to upset you, Mom. Let's just go home, please."

Gina got out, slammed the door, and tottered to her car with her stilettos sticking in the uneven gravel.

Anna Beth drove away without looking in her rearview mirror. She was halfway home when the thought came: *I have really made a mess of things. But there's no way I could have this conversation in a crowded restaurant. What if Mom doesn't show? It would not be unlike her. She almost missed my graduation. If she doesn't show, then she'll find out when she finds out.*

———•———

Looking at the clock every five minutes, Anna Beth stayed dressed, waiting, and hoping. She told herself she wouldn't get the food out until her mom showed up, but after an hour she figured her mom wasn't coming. She didn't want to be alone, and Alicia had invited her to her graduation party. But Anna Beth knew a laughter-filled family celebration would make her sadness unbearable. She was incapable of pasting on a smile today and didn't want to inflict her mood on anyone else, so she decided to slip into shorts and one of John's T-shirts and eat alone.

Anna Beth was buttering a slice of artisan bread to toast when the doorbell rang. She looked at the kitchen clock. Six fifteen.

She opened the door to find her mom, almost breathless, still in stilettos, and holding two gift-wrapped boxes. "Mom, I thought you weren't coming." The relief she felt surprised her, although she didn't know if it was relief that she wouldn't be alone or relief that she would get to deliver her news as she had planned. More than needing her mom's compassion, she needed to hear and see her mom's response to the news and what that might mean for her future and the baby's.

"I didn't want to leave with you still mad at me." Her mother walked in. Like always, Gina brought trinkets to try to make amends.

"I'm not mad at you, Mom. I only wanted to come home and have a quiet meal with just the two of us." Anna Beth closed the door.

"Look. I stopped and got you a couple of graduation gifts. I think you'll really like them." Her mom teetered to the living room, ankles wobbling as she tried to balance the packages. They practically slid out of her arms onto the sofa. She sat down next to the boxes and pulled off her shoes. "Oh, my aching feet. I bought these shoes and this outfit just for your graduation. I thought these shoes were the prettiest things I've ever seen, and they make my calves look good. Don't you think so?"

Anna Beth went along, remembering she'd worn one of her mom's outdated skirts and a blouse for graduation. No new outfit for her. "They're real pretty, Mom, and your legs always look good. Probably not so good for walking, though."

Gina rubbed her tanned ankles and feet and well-manicured toes. "Here, open your presents. You wouldn't believe it. When I was shopping, I ran into a nurse. I told her I was shopping for my girl who had just graduated with honors and might be going to nursing school. Then I asked her what she would suggest as a good graduation gift for someone planning to be a nurse."

Anna Beth said, "Uh . . . Mom, I need to talk to you about that."

Gina almost whined, "Not now. Not before you open your presents."

Anna Beth complied. She removed the wrapping to find a box showing a picture of a slow cooker. She couldn't imagine any other eighteen-year-old graduate receiving a convenient kitchen appliance as her only graduation gift. "That's nice, Mom."

Gina looked at her manicured nails and tanned hands as she talked. "Yes. The nurse said that you would be so busy, and a slow cooker would be your salvation." She pointed to the other box. "Keep opening."

Anna Beth opened the smaller box to find a pair of clunky-looking black clogs. She lifted them from the box. "A pair of shoes. I haven't had a new pair in quite a while."

"Not just any shoes. These are special shoes that nurses wear. Supposed to be comfortable and good for your feet and legs when you're standing all day. You know how I am about shoes, so I got a pair of hot-pink ones for myself too. My job keeps me on my feet all day, too, but I didn't want any black ones. I got you black because you'll be a nurse and all."

"Thank you." Anna Beth did her best to hide her disappointment. She knew her mom meant well. "I've tossed some greens, and I was about to toast the bread to go with the lobster salad I made. And I got a cake—a real bakery cake with decorations. Chocolate with buttercream icing—your favorite."

"Oh, girl. I don't need food. What I need now is a foot rub." Gina moved the slow cooker box to the floor, turned herself to a reclining position. She pointed to the other end of the sofa. "Sit there and give your mom a foot rub like you used to do."

Anna Beth did as asked, thinking this was a good time to talk. "Okay, we can eat later." She began to massage her mom's feet and noticed how much they looked like hers. "Mom, there's something I need to talk to you about."

"Okay, Sugar Pie, you talk away. I'm listening with my eyes closed."

Somehow it was easier for Anna Beth to talk when her mother wasn't looking at her. "Mom, I'm not sure I'll be going to nursing school."

"Well, that's okay. You just do whatever suits you best. You still have the job at the supermarket, or if you want to come up to Hilton Head, I'll see if I can find you a job at the resort."

Anna Beth would have been wringing her hands if she hadn't been massaging Gina's feet. "It's not that I don't want to go to nursing school. I've always wanted to be a nurse, but . . . but, Mom, there's just no easy way to tell you this so I'll just say it. I'm pregnant."

Gina's eyes opened wide, and she jerked herself to a sitting position as though the room had just been struck by lightning. "What? You're pregnant? Who's the father?" She squinched her eyes and took a deep, disapproving breath.

The cry in Anna Beth's voice was that of a wounded animal. "I can't believe you'd ask me that. There's never been anyone but John. You know I loved him. We were engaged, and it was only one time—the night before he left for the oil rig."

Gina's eyes shifted from side to side while she calculated. "That means you're already four months pregnant? I think you can still get rid of it. That's exactly what you need to do."

Anna Beth stood from the couch. She raised her voice. "Not an option. I can't believe you think I would do that."

"And I can't believe you'd do this to me. Getting pregnant. I told you when you turned fifteen I'd get you birth-control pills, but no, you never asked. No excuse for this. One time, and you're pregnant. What are the chances of that?" Gina was putting her stilettos back on.

"I didn't need birth-control pills when I was fifteen, Mom. It was one time, no matter what you think. John was always so respectful, and he had just asked me to marry him that night, and he was leaving. Yeah, what are the chances? All I can say is that this baby must have been meant to be. If John were alive, he would take care of me and the baby."

Gina stood. "Well, he's not alive, is he? He's dead. So, who do think is going to take care of you and this baby? And don't look at me. I had you young, and your daddy married me, but he was no help. Worse than no help, and you know that. I would have been better off alone. I'm telling you like my mama told me, 'You made your bed, now lie in it.' And I can tell you from experience, it's a hard, hard bed you've made for yourself."

Anna Beth's eyes filled with tears, and her stomach heaved. She had her answers. There would be no help, no support, no compassion from her mom. Only disdain. "I'm sorry if I disappointed you, Mom. I truly am. And I'm sorry if giving birth to me made your life miserable and hard. You just go on about your life, and maybe it'll be better that way. I'll handle my life and my hard bed."

She felt her mom's icy stare as they stood face to face.

"Not going to nursing school? I can understand that. So, what are you going to do?"

"I don't know. That's why I wanted to talk to you. But I'll be okay. You don't need to worry." *I've always been okay despite you.* "I'll make it because I must. I have a human being who is depending on me, and I will do whatever is necessary to give this baby a good upbringing and a chance at a decent life."

Gina grabbed her purse.

Anna Beth moved from where she stood in front of the sofa. "Are you leaving now, before we eat? I have a lot of questions that I hoped you could answer. I have no one else talk to about what it's like being pregnant and giving birth."

"Well, find yourself a doctor if you're determined to go through with this. I hope you find some answers to your questions. I was never good at that anyway. I have to go. I told you Rodney expects me by eleven."

"And what if you're not there by eleven?"

"I won't be finding that out. Besides, I cannot deal with any more of this now. I come all this way to celebrate your graduation, and this is the thanks I get."

Gina walked straight to the front door as if she were an arrow aimed at a target. She was out and gone without so much as a nod or a goodbye.

Anna Beth was too stunned to cry. She slumped to the sofa, holding her head in her hands. After a moment she looked at the black clogs in the box on the floor. For some unknown reason, she picked up one of the shoes and turned it over to look inside. Size eight and a half. She wore a size six, and her mom didn't even know it. But she now knew what she needed to know. Her mom had answered with great clarity and with only a few words—even the questions that went unasked. In her heart of hearts, Anna Beth had known the answers all along, and her mom had confirmed it.

Anna Beth was alone in the world.

Chapter Seven

———— ♦ ————

Saturday, December 6
Savannah, Georgia

S tuart and Jillian had started a Christmas tradition their first Christmas as a married couple, and now fourteen years later, they made their annual trip to Savannah for a weekend with their boys. Savannah was an enchanting city any time of the year, but it was nothing less than magical at Christmastime—Christmas carolers in period costumes, the decorated historical homes, the lights, and festive delicacies to please the palate. No snow-laden limbs of conifer trees or swags of flocked, fake fir branches. Instead, ancient oaks tinseled in Spanish moss and twinkling lights and fresh wreaths made of magnolia leaves and holly berries and feathered with pine made for a southern Christmas.

It had been a cooler day than usual, and the heavy gray clouds hovered over the city as the O'Haras took an Old Town trolley ride through the historical district and visited the Christmas Market. The day had been gray enough that residents kept the candles in their windows lit for the visitors and passersby to enjoy.

The family had enjoyed a stroll along the riverfront, and the boys had consumed more candy than they were normally allowed. But it was Christmas. Every baker and confectioner offered samples, and Reese and Riley were gifted in eyeing them. They spent well over half an hour in River Street Sweets and left with several bags: pralines, sea-salted chocolate caramels, glazed pecans, peanut-butter chocolate-swirl fudge, pecan divinity, and Jillian's favorite, a pecan log roll. Treats to last through Christmas with gift tins for friends.

However, the shopping stopped when the chocolate-caramel apples caught Riley's eye. Reese, the careful one, chose toffee. But not Riley. He wanted the apple, and when the young clerk took one from the case, Riley had her return it for a larger one almost the size of his head. Stuart and Jillian relished occupying a bench along the river to observe the shoppers and tourists who seemed a bit more joyful than usual and to be entertained by their young son with a chocolate-caramel disaster on a stick.

It had taken young Riley more than half an hour to eat his treat. Most of it made it to his mouth, but in the wrestling match, chocolate and caramel coated his jacket. Riley won, eating every bite down to the apple's core and making it a production while Reese sat quietly next to his parents and ate only one piece of toffee.

They returned to their hotel suite after a full day of sightseeing. Stuart sat with his legs crossed in the lounge chair next to the window. Riley was perched on his father's foot as if it were a rocking horse, and every few seconds, Stuart would give Riley a jolt by lifting his leg. The sound of Riley's innocent laughter always softened Jillian's heart.

Reese stood at the window overlooking the river. Jillian

asked, "Tell me, Reese, what was your favorite thing we did today?"

He did not move but continued his gaze out through the glass panes. "The trolley ride and the art gallery on River Street. Thank you for buying me the book. It will give me lots of ideas about things to paint."

"You're welcome. I enjoyed that stop too. Sorry you and Riley missed it, Stuart, but we knew you two would have more fun somewhere else, like the toy shop. I could have done some damage to our budget in the art gallery, especially with things I imagined for the carriage house. But then I thought, *I don't need a one of those paintings. I'll just tell Reese what I'd like him to paint.* How blessed we are to have a real artist in the family—a gift passed down through the generations."

Riley squealed when his dad bolted his leg. "I might be an artist one day when I get big like Reese."

Jillian smiled. "Yes, you just might. So, tell me, Riley, what was your favorite thing about today? And a chocolate-covered caramel apple does not count."

"No fair. Apples should count. I liked the trolley, but nobody was driving. I kept looking for the driver." Riley paused and crawled into his dad's lap. "But I really, really, really wanted to go see the ghosts that man was talking about. Real scary houses."

"There's no such thing as ghosts, Riley," Reese quickly snapped.

"Is too. That man said that Christmas ghosts live in those big old houses, and they come out at night."

Reese, the practical one, said, "That man was just trying to sell tickets for tonight's walking tour of the Ghosts of Christmas."

Riley pouted at his dad. "Why didn't you get us tickets?"

Stuart replied calmly. "Because your brother's right. No such thing as ghosts. Buying tickets and expecting to see ghosts would be like buying your chocolate-caramel apple this afternoon only to find out there was no apple inside. They'd only tell us some stories about imaginary ghosts and explain why they didn't show up."

Reese added, "And besides, you'd be so scared your curly red hair would turn into white fuzz, and you'd be climbing into bed with me after one of your bad dreams."

"I would not. I'm not scared of ghosts. And it would have been all right if my apple was only chocolate and caramel. And ghosts are real. We saw that movie about that mean, stingy man, and the ghosts came to visit him at Christmas because he wasn't being kind."

"Just a movie, son," Stuart replied.

Jillian saw Stuart roll his eyes. "Your dad's right. That was just a movie, and movies are not real."

"Yes, they are. I saw a movie about Davy Crockett, and he was real."

Jillian realized this conversation was going nowhere. "Enough talk about ghosts and movies. Want to know what my favorite part of the day was?"

Riley giggled. "Holding Dad's hand. I saw you kiss him too."

"Well, that's close. My favorite part of the day was being with my guys—my favorite people in the whole wide world." She looked at her watch. "We should be getting ready for dinner. We need to leave in about half an hour."

"Where we goin'?" Riley asked.

Stuart shook his head. "Did all that chocolate coat your brain so you can't remember, son? For the third time, we're going to Tybee Island to have dinner with the Lamberts. Mr. Lambert is an old family friend, and he's invited us to celebrate Christmas Gullah style with them tonight. It will be a new cultural experience for you boys."

Riley was curious. "What's Gullah mean, Dad? I don't think it sounds very nice. Will there be any kids?"

Jillian grinned and patted her husband's shoulder on her way to the bedroom. "Good luck with that one."

She heard Stuart as she left the room.

"I'll tell you all about the Gullah people while we're driving. This horse is tired, Riley. Hop down. And go wash your face and comb your hair. I'll bring your clothes for dinner. You, too, Reese. Navy pants, white shirt, and the green Christmas sweaters your mom got for you."

Twenty minutes later, Jillian was the first one to the door, dressed in her go-to for a Christmas dinner: black skirt, white silk blouse, pearls, and her favorite hand-painted silk scarf with Christmas greenery, holly, and magnolias. Stuart looked preppy in his camel-colored pants, sky-blue shirt, and navy blazer, and the boys had on navy pants with emerald-green cable-knit sweaters over white shirts. Preppy like their dad. Jillian had wanted red sweaters for the boys, but Reese had resisted, claiming freckle-faced boys with red curls didn't need red sweaters.

Jillian stood admiring her guys and checking for any mishaps, especially in the untamable-hair department. "Okay, gentleman—especially you two." She eyed her sons. "Remember, we are guests in the Lamberts' home tonight. There will be no other children, and I expect you boys to remember all that we've been practicing the last couple of weeks—your table manners, no loud talking, no comment-ing on the food unless you say it's delicious, no eye rolling or squirming. And remember: napkins. And the most important: use only gracious words. I want the Lamberts to close their door when we leave tonight and say to each other, 'Those boys will be fine young men someday.'" She looked at Riley. "Do we need to go over the gracious words again?"

Riley surprised her. "Heck, no, Mom. I got 'em."

Her eyes widened as she pinched his ear and frowned to keep from grinning. "Riley Callahan O'Hara, *heck* is not a gracious word, and I don't ever want to hear it come out of your mouth again. Where did you hear that?"

"Jake says it all the time."

Stuart stepped in. "Well, that had better be the last time you say it. Now get your jackets, boys, and let's go."

———•———

Stuart settled into the driver's seat and turned the key. "Everyone buckled up? We're about to ride."

Riley started in before they were out of the parking garage. "Is it long to get there?"

"About eighteen miles, and it'll take us about thirty minutes. Show him when it will be seven o'clock on your watch, Reese." Stuart was proud that his son wore his gramps' watch and that it wasn't digital. "Do you remember coming to Tybee Island when you were about five?"

"I remember some things. Is that the beach where we found the shells and the sand dollars?"

"You do remember." Stuart chuckled. "And you didn't understand why we couldn't take the sand dollars home. Gramps and Granny O used to bring your uncle Connor and me to Tybee Island for a week every summer. We fished and swam, and Granny O walked the beaches in search of shells to add to her collection."

Riley asked, "You mean her shells in the glass case at the library?"

"The very ones. Granny O donated her collection to the library so that other people could enjoy them."

"You boys come from good people," Jillian added.

"Your grandparents were always about doing good. Gramps helped Mr. Lambert get started in business many years ago, and your dad has continued to work with him as his accountant."

"Dad, what does that word mean? You know the word you said?"

Stuart looked in the rearview mirror to see Riley holding Reese's wrist, staring at his watch as if the hand wouldn't move if he weren't looking. No doubt Reese had told him the long hand was the one to watch. "That word would be *Gullah*. You hear a lot about the Gullah or Geechee people in this neck of the woods. They came from Africa as slaves a few hundred years ago—not by their choice but because they were captured and sold. You see, this area all around is known as plantation country, and the slaves were brought here to work as farmhands on the plantations. The Gullah people were wise about farming. But when President Abraham Lincoln freed the slaves—"

Riley interrupted. "I know President Lincoln. He wore a funny hat, and he never told a lie. I mean a fib."

Stuart chuckled. "That's a good start, Riley. When the slaves were freed and no longer owned by their masters, they had no home, no land, no education, and no way to provide for their families. So, the plantation owners gave them the marshlands out on these islands. It was the worst land they had, but the Gullah people took it and began to grown rice and indigo."

"Are the Gullah people 'mericans?"

Stuart chuckled at his son's literal understanding and curiosity. "Of course they are Americans. Mr. Lambert's great-great-grandparents were slaves who were freed, and the Gullah traditions were passed on to him by his grandparents and parents. Tonight, we're having a Gullah Christmas dinner, and he and Mrs. Lambert have promised to tell us about the Gullah ways."

Reese was smug. "Sounds like history class to me."

Jillian responded quickly. "A bit of history, but more important, a delicious, cultural experience."

Riley inquired, "What's a cultural?"

"Culture in someone's way of life. It's what we believe about life," Jillian answered. "The language we speak, our art and music, and even our food are all part of our culture. Since we can't go to Africa tonight, aren't we fortunate to experience a bit of the African culture with a Gullah dinner?"

"Depends on what's for dinner," Reese mumbled.

Jillian turned to look at her son. "I heard that, Reese. I've enjoyed Mrs. Lambert's cooking, and you will too. And even if you don't, you will act like it. Is that understood?"

"Yes, ma'am. No feeding the dog under the table."

Stuart secretly smiled and slowed the car. "Wish it was daylight so you boys could see the island. We're about to cross the Lazaretto Creek Bridge, which connects the island to the mainland. This is the mouth of the Savannah River. You know the river that we can see out the hotel window? That's the Savannah. It starts up north of here where North Carolina, South Carolina, and Georgia meet, and it just lazily flows all the way to right here where it enters the Atlantic Ocean."

Reese spoke up. "So, we're getting a history lesson, a Gullah cultural experience, and a geography lesson, and we don't have to read about it in a book. We're living it."

Stuart chuckled. "Now, I can expand the history lesson by telling you that General Oglethorpe landed on these shores in the mid-1700s with over a hundred passengers. They came up the river and founded a colony that became our state of Georgia."

"Named for King George, the king of England at the

time," Reese added. "And Dad, the people Oglethorpe brought with him were former prisoners. They were in prison because they couldn't pay their bills. Putting people in jail because they can't pay their bills makes no sense to me."

"Well, son, you could be right about that, and you seem to remember some things I've forgotten since my Georgia history class. And the Lazaretto Bridge we crossed? That word *lazaretto* means a place where people were quarantined in case they were sick or diseased. Could have been a ship or a hospital or an island like this one. Interesting to think that folks were quarantined on this island that's now some of the most expensive land in these parts." Stuart made a right turn. "We're almost there and right on time."

Riley squealed. "Yep. That's what Reese's watch says. The long hand's on twelve."

Stuart parked the car, went around, and opened the door for Jillian. Both boys were already out of the car. Stuart took Riley's hand after he helped to put his shirt tail back in. "Remember, boys, what your mom taught you. Napkins. Good manners. And gracious words."

———•———

The Lamberts' low-country house was as inviting as the Lamberts were jolly. Jillian knew them to be joyful people year-round, not just at Christmas. It had been a few years since she had been in their home. She admired the spacious dwelling, filled with vibrant color and beachy, comfortable furniture that made you want to sit a spell. She imagined how the large windows would be open in the summertime to allow the sea breezes to cool the house. Tonight the skies had cleared, and the windows were eyes to visible stars flickering over the shimmering water just yards away. The

Christmas decorations using Spanish moss and pinecones were unusual. Indigo was the prominent color in all Mrs. Lambert's ornaments and décor. Nothing, not even the decorated tree, included the traditional red-and-green plaid used at the O'Haras' house.

When Jillian inquired about the many sweetgrass baskets on shelves and tables, and larger ones on the floor, Mrs. Lambert explained. "These were hand-made by the Gullah and Geechee artists who learned the art passed down through the generations." She picked up a basket and handed it to Jillian. "You'll see these are not like the typical woven baskets of the Native Americans, but long strands of grass coiled in the tradition of the African basket makers. And the blue ones were dyed using the indigo the Gullah people grew, harvested, and made into paint and dye right here in the islands."

The word *paint* captured Reese's attention. Jillian was pleased when Reese inquired about the folk art that speckled the room with primary colors and asked Mrs. Lambert for permission to walk around and look at the primitive paintings and the seascapes. Jillian followed Mrs. Lambert as she gave Reese a tour through the entire house, showing him the works of her favorite Geechee artists. She was amazed that her son could speak so intelligently of light, space, energy, and contrasts. Reese had out the small pad and pencil he always kept in his pocket. Jillian didn't know if he was making notes or sketching.

Reese commented, "You said these were Geechee artists. Is there a difference between Geechee and Gullah people?"

Mrs. Lambert's eyes lit up. "Very insightful question, young man. The Gullah and Geechee people came from West Africa, and they are similar in their culture. They're called Gullah along the coast of the Carolinas, and we call them Geechee here in Georgia. And these days, they're both working to keep their culture alive."

Mrs. Lambert finished her tour. "Reese, you may continue to look around if you'd like. It pleases me so much that you find our art collection interesting. I've already heard from your dad that you're quite an artist yourself. Maybe one day soon one of your paintings will find a home here."

Jillian watched Reese's freckled face flush.

"Oh, he is quite good," she said. "And what an honor it would be for one of his works to hang in your home."

"Come, Jillian, I must go to the kitchen. Everything is ready, but it's time to get the food on the table."

Jillian followed. "I've been eager to ask about your dress. It is stunning."

Mrs. Lambert chuckled. "'Stunning'? Well, that's a nice word to say it's loud. I chose it because it is so colorful. It's a dashiki, native to West Africa." She twirled around. "It flows with the wind and hides the abundance of what I have eaten in my lifetime." She laughed again.

The parade of dishes started as everyone took seats at the glass-topped table with bamboo legs. As Mrs. Lambert served, she noted the Geechee and Gullah people's strong connection to the land and the vegetables they grew and explained the significance of everything she served. "First, we're having our salad. Watermelon is a favorite fruit and easy to grow in the islands. You're having a watermelon and heirloom tomato salad, followed by okra soup laced with three kinds of peppers and smoked chicken wings. Now, after the soup, your palate may need a little cooling off. So, I'll tame the spiciness with a watermelon granita before I serve the main course of oyster and shrimp perlou." Mrs. Lambert's wide, toothy smile, sparkling against her caramel-colored skin, showed her pleasure in appearing with each new course.

"Now, for those who haven't developed a taste for oysters and shrimp cooked in rice and onions, I'll be bringing out a chicken bog—one like my *bibi* made with chicken, sausage, more rice and onions, and some flavorful African spices. She was my granny and the one who taught me to cook." She disappeared again, returning with another taurine in one hand and a basket of hot, sliced cornbread in the other. "You all get started. Tom, why don't you serve their plates. These dishes are hot and heavy. I'll be back with the collard and turnip greens in just a moment."

Jillian observed, hoping that she could be as jolly a hostess as Mrs. Lambert when it came time to celebrate Christmas at the O'Haras'.

Mrs. Lambert reappeared with a large bowl of greens and finally took her seat at the end of the table. "Now, if you were eating at my *bibi's* house, you'd have sweet potatoes, but I've put them in the bread pudding for dessert." She looked at Riley. "I'm guessing you'd like a scoop of ice cream on your bread pudding, Riley."

"Heck, yeah."

Jillian just closed her eyes. Should she reprimand him? Or should she just swallow the sausage in her mouth and let it go?

Mrs. Lambert's belly rippled under her dashiki when she laughed. "Heck, yeah. Me too."

The meal was a more than a cultural experience. Delectable food. Laughter. Stories. They became family around the table. As the evening was ending, Mrs. Lambert handed Reese a pewter candle snuffer and asked him to extinguish the candles on the table and the ones in the windows. Then she put her hand on his and said, "All the candles go out at the close of the day, except the Christ candle with the nativity scene on the mantle. We keep it burning during Christmas, just like we keep it burning in our hearts all year long."

Jillian thought it indeed a beautiful evening, especially when they were saying their goodbyes and Riley went so naturally to hug the Lamberts—a hug like he had given Gramps and Granny O.

At the door, Mr. Lambert handed each of the boys a small handsewn bag made of indigo-colored African fabric and filled with an assortment of hard candies. He explained this was what he'd gotten for Christmas as a child. Then Mrs. Lambert gave Jillian a sweetgrass breadbasket, one she would use with pride on her Christmas dinner table, hoping that her Christmas guests would leave her home as happy and satisfied as Mrs. Lambert had made them feel tonight.

It was a quiet drive back to the hotel. Both boys were asleep before they got to the bridge. Jillian enjoyed gazing at the night sky away from the city lights. She reflected on Christmas, its cultural traditions that were different and yet the same. Traditions that brought people together to celebrate the event that had changed human history. She was committed to making Christmas more meaningful around their table this year.

Chapter Eight

Saturday, December 13
Bar Haven

Rosemary, the pastor's wife, held fast to the hood on her rain jacket, trying to keep her regular Saturday-morning visit to the beauty shop for tight, bluish-purple curls preserved for Sunday morning. Jillian rushed to keep up with her as they approached the back entrance to the church. "Winds a-howling this morning."

Jillian took Rosemary's arm up the steps. "I'm waiting for it to blow some warmer weather in. Looks like some of the ladies are already here. I see the lights on in Fellowship Hall."

Rosemary opened the door. "I'm glad for it. Jenny's making coffee, and Sylvia volunteered to bring her Christmas-morning apple-cinnamon muffins. Can't have a meeting without some eating, you know, especially at Christmas."

Minutes later, the committee ladies were seated around

a table, and Rosemary was wiping the last crumb of muffin from her chin and emptying her coffee cup. She had barely swallowed before she began talking.

"Is there anything better than Christmas?" She chuckled. "We've been having Christmas all year getting ready for this event, and ladies, if I could kick my heels together like I could forty years ago, I'd be doing it this morning. You all have worked hard for months getting everything and everyone ready for our live Christmas nativity for this year. Now, I've been having those feelings I get when I just know something right and special is about to happen. I don't get goose bumps, I get glory bumps when I have this kind of inkling. And I can tell this morning that my skin's been looking like a de-feathered Christmas turkey. I'm sure this will become one of Bar Haven's Christmas traditions that'll have people driving from far and near to see, and I have a feeling this year will be one to remember. Can you just imagine all the children that will be so excited to see what we have planned and made happen?"

Jillian watched the ladies nod and smile on cue as if it had been choreographed. "Oh, I think people of all ages will enjoy it, but if Riley, my youngest, is a barometer for excitement, then our work will have been an investment in children, to be sure."

Rosemary continued. "I like that word *investment*. And I especially like investments that have huge payoffs. God's grace and heaven are big payoffs." She looked down at her open notebook. "Okay, we're one week away. Let's go through our checklist. Linda, can you tell us where we are on the costumes?"

"Costumes are made, pressed, and packaged better than my Christmas fruitcake that's been aging since Thanksgiving. Shades of blue for Mary, Joseph in shades of brown, swaddling for the baby, three shepherds and one shepherd boy in rugged attire, and three Wise Men in purple and gold. Each costume is different, and they all look authentic. We only hope the men have their own sandals. And if this weather keeps up, they'll be wearing socks too." Linda bowed her head briefly and then looked up. "And one more thing. You remember we were planning to borrow some fancy crowns for the Wise Men. That's not going to happen."

Rosemary frowned. "Not going to happen? What are you planning to do? Don't you think the wise men need crowns?"

Linda smiled, looking pleased. "And they will have them. We went to Savannah to look at the crowns, only to discover they were more like turbans. So, we came home and made our own. You know how it is around here when there's a need. The money just appeared for the fancy fabric and gold braiding and even a few shiny baubles. They're beautiful, and they're ours to be used for years to come. That is, unless Manny wears his out before Christmas. He's already chosen his and has been entertaining the kids wearing it around the house telling them how wise it makes him feel."

Rosemary chortled. "Would that all our men were as willing as your Manny is to put on a costume and stand still for three hours. Getting these guys to volunteer was worse than giving a cat a bath. But it's finally done. The only character we're missing is the Baby Jesus. I've been praying since January that we'd have a real-life baby in that manger, but my granddaughter's lifelike baby doll is the best I could do. I'll get the doll to you midweek, Linda, so you can get it swaddled properly." She looked down at her notes again. "Suellen, where are we on the construction of the crèche? I think I saw some framing as I was driving in."

Suellen responded. "Roger and the guys came yesterday

afternoon and put up the structure in the perfect spot on the edge of the property. They were planning to work today until the rains came, but they might be able to finish up this afternoon. Their plan is to get the framing done, cover the top with chicken wire, and add the grasses, palmetto branches, and hay next Friday. They want it fresh and dry. Oh, and they've run electricity out there because they plan to hang up a shining start in the oak tree above the manger scene. I'm happy to say that Roger had no trouble getting Mr. Buckingham and a couple of other gentlemen to help him. It'll be done just as planned. Now we need to add sunshine to our prayer list."

"Well, we have costumes and characters and a crèche. What about the animals, Jillian?"

"Reese has finished all the painting, and the camel and sheep are corralled in our carriage house. Buck's coming by on Monday to help Reese and Stuart put on the hinges. Then they'll be ready for moving to the church. Their plan is to do that on a sunny day and put them in the storage unit behind the church until time to set up."

"I'm sure Reese did a good job. But what happens if they get wet?"

"They'll be fine. Reese used good oil-based paint and then sealed them. I must say they look amazingly real. They are life sized, and you can see the hairs on the camel's two humps and the whiskers on the donkey. Reese accepted the challenge, and he came through. The sheep look so real, our visitors will expect them to say 'baa-baa.'"

They ladies giggled as Rosemary added, "And it's a relief that we won't have to feed them or clean up after them." She turned to Sylvia and Jenny, who were seated next to each other. "That leaves the refreshments. You ladies are known for what delights come out of your kitchen, but I do hope you didn't take it all upon yourselves to feed our guests from four counties for this event."

Sylvia spoke first. "Yes, ma'am. We are not quite ready yet, but we will be come next Saturday." She looked at Jenny. "Jenny's freezer is full of the things we could make ahead, and we'll be finishing up with the baking on Friday morning. You've taught us about involving people and delegating, and that's what we did. Lucky for us that our ladies are generous and gracious with their kitchen skills."

Jenny added, "Three teams of them. They not only took responsibility for the treats Sylvia and I suggested, they came up with some of their own favorites. A Christmas dessert smorgasbord is what we're having. And enough wassail and hot chocolate to float a flotilla."

"And dishes?" Rosemary asked.

"Paper goods, ma'am. Beautiful matching Christmas napkins and plates. Nothing much to clean up. Except you know these ladies. They'll be bringing out their silver trays that have been in the back of the cupboard since last Christmas. Better get ready. There'll be a stampede for silver polish at the supermarket this week. But that's how we do things in Bar Haven. We will make you proud, Miss Rosemary. We promise."

"I have no doubt." Rosemary pulled another sheet from her notebook. "It wouldn't be Christmas without music. Of course, we'll have our regular Christmas concert on Sunday evening with handbells, a brass quintet, our glorious choir, and our organ that needs some work. A fine pipe organ would not choose to live in Bar Haven with this warm, moist air we enjoy almost year-round. We're just grateful to have an organ even if it is cantankerous." Rosemary raised both arms. "And the Ding-Dongs are ready, and I might add a 'Praise the Lord' to that. And please don't tell them what I called them. The handbell choir will be there to play Christmas carols for the live nativity Sunday evening, and it wouldn't be Christmas if Irma Crenshaw didn't sing the song that made her famous around these parts. She'll use her autoharp for accompaniment. Everyone is well rehearsed, and barring a siege of the flu like the one that nearly wiped us out four years ago, we are good to go. And it will be glorious."

Jillian raised her hand. "Will we be hearing something glorious from you this year?"

Rosemary shook her head. "Only from the organ for the concert and Christmas Eve. No one, and I mean no one, enjoys an old, warbling soprano. Besides I'm the only one brave enough to tackle that organ. I know its quirks, and it knows mine. We're old friends, and we still have a few Christmases left in us."

"I'm sorry to hear that you won't be singing. No one sings 'O Holy Night' like you. At least, you'll be leading our children for the Christmas Eve service. You're the only reason I can get Reese and Riley to be a part of that. I don't know if it's the M&M's you give them, or if they don't want to miss what antic you might pull at rehearsal. All I know is my children love you, and so do we. Don't we, ladies?"

All the ladies stood and clapped.

"And I love y'all too. Just let me know if anything changes or if you need my help. This Christmas will be glorious, and all our work will be an investment—an investment in people's lives and eternities. That's what Christmas is all about. Oh, we've all been at work, but our real job is to make sure heaven is a crowded place. Don't want anyone to miss that. Meeting adjourned."

Rosemary picked up her notebook, put her thumb and index finger between her lips, and let out a whistle that would have alerted someone at the lighthouse out on the point. "Sylvia, if there's another apple muffin left, I'm fairly certain it has my name on it." Her unmistakable cackle filled the room.

Later Saturday afternoon
The O'Haras' house

The previous few days had kept Jillian busy finishing the carriage house and decorating for Christmas, but she saved the two trees for Saturday afternoon. Decorating the trees together was another of their family Christmas traditions. She was currently in the living room unpacking boxes of Christmas ornaments and waiting for Stuart and the boys to get home to start dressing the trees.

Stuart had secured the large fir in front of the picture window in the living room while she was at the church earlier this morning, but he needed something from the hardware store to secure the tree in the gathering room. Saturday just wasn't Saturday if he didn't make his weekly trip to the local hardware store. But she figured it was Christmas, and her boys might have some shopping to do that did not include her, so she didn't mind their absence.

Christmas music reverberated through the whole house. The storage bins were open, and the living-room floor was scattered with smaller boxes of ornaments, all packed according to color.

She sat on the sofa and opened the box of crocheted angel ornaments Granny O had made and given to her and Stuart for their first Christmas. Each angel, crafted from the finest cotton thread, had taken over eight hours to crochet. Their halos were dotted with iridescent seed pearls. Granny O had explained how she threaded fifteen pearls onto her crocheting thread and pulled each one up individually and secured it as she crocheted the halos. Then the limp, lifeless-looking angels had to be sized, shaped, and starched to look like angels. Jillian treasured them. When it was time, she would divide them and pass them on to her sons and their families.

With the unpacking done, she did a walk-through of the house while she waited for her guys to get home. There wasn't a flat surface in the downstairs rooms that didn't look like Christmas: tables with nativity scenes, crystal bowls of mercury-glass ornaments, pinecone-filled baskets tied with red and green plaid ribbons, red and green candles that smelled of Christmas. She had spent all of Thursday making garlands of coastal pine and southern magnolia leaves entwined with smaller sweet magnolia and laced with magnolia seed pods. She was fortunate that her backyard was as much of a treasure chest of green foliage for Christmas as Gramps' boxes had been for the heirloom decorations for the family tree. Fresh garland lined the staircase, and wreaths of it hung in the front windows facing the street— all eight of them. Having enjoyed the candles in the windows of Savannah's historic homes, she put candles protected by hurricane glasses in each of the windows. Now to keep Riley from setting the house on fire . . .

She walked into the dining room. Stacks of her ruby-red dishes and glassware used only for Christmas and Valentine's Day lined the sideboard. Too early to set the Christmas table. That would come next weekend. But she had set the breakfast table in the kitchen with Christmas dishes and Christmas candles. That was her place to practice with her boys for Christmas dinner with the family.

She was searching the sideboard drawers for her favorite Christmas napkins when she heard Stuart and the boys come through the back door. Within seconds, the Christmas music had been turned down. She heard Stuart hollering.

"Jilly, what's with the Christmas music? We could hear

trumpets playing 'Joy to the World' all the way to the filling station."

She joined them in the kitchen. "That's good. I hope it gave everyone a joyful heart. Hop on the stools at the bar in the kitchen. Snack time, boys, and then on to decorating the Christmas trees. I have everything unpacked."

Riley squirmed on the stool while Jillian poured two glasses of cold milk and brought out the cookies. "I got you a present, Mama."

Reese turned to Riley. "If you say something, I'm going wire your teeth together so you can't open your mouth."

Riley quickly said, "But I'm notta telling you what it is."

"Good. I'd rather wait until Christmas morning for it to be a surprise." She handed them each two cookies. "These are the World's Best Cookies according to Nana."

"Did she have to eat every cookie in the world to find out?" Riley took a bite.

"I don't think so. But it's Nana's recipe, and it's what she named them. We had them every Christmas when I was growing up. I would help Nana in the kitchen when she made them. My job was to crush the cornflakes." Jillian took a bite of cookie. "Umm. Nana's right. World's Best Cookie."

Thirty minutes later, the tiny white lights were strung and laced with silver tinsel, and the silver and gold mercury-glass balls and bells were hung. Jillian asked the boys to help with Granny O's crocheted angels.

"Just perch each one so that we can see them from the inside. The people passing by will get to enjoy all the sparkles and the lights, but we get to enjoy Granny O's angels."

Stuart put the star on top, and Riley plugged in the lights.

Jillian stood back and admired the elegant tree. "Magazine worthy. Okay, we're done with the fancy one. I'll pack away the boxes and bins later. Let's get on to the fun family tree in the gathering room."

"Want me to unplug the lights, Mom?" Riley asked.

"Let's leave them on and let the people walking or driving by enjoy them, just like we did in Savannah last weekend. It will be our Christmas gift to the community, especially if your dad will turn the volume of our Christmas music back up."

Riley followed Jillian through the kitchen into the gathering room. "Dad was just teasin' you, Mama. Mr. Griff was playing loud music at the filling station. We could hear it all over town."

"Then let's turn ours up just a smidgen and get started."

Stuart had secured the perfectly shaped blue spruce in the corner next to the fireplace. It filled the space and could be seen through the window facing the side street. No tiny white lights on this tree. Stuart had already wrapped the tree from top to bottom in old-fashioned large bulbs in primary colors. Jillian handed each of the boys the bins with their names on them. "Here are your ornaments. One for each year you've been on this planet. You two go first, then your dad and I will put our special ornaments on the tree. And then a surprise."

"That's not fair. Reese has more than me," Riley whined.

Reese responded. "I'm the oldest. I'll always have more, but I'll share with you. Take what you'd like." He extended his box to Riley.

When the tree was covered in handcrafted baubles made of everything from Styrofoam cups to popsicle sticks that made picture frames for the boys' Christmas pictures, Jillian and Stuart put on their prized ornaments. Then she pulled out the box she had found in Gramps' closet.

"Look, boys, these ornaments are so special. Your great-grandmother made Christmas ornaments for Gramps when he was growing up. She painted an ornament each year until Gramps turned eighteen and got married. These will go on our family tree for the first time. Just think, we have Granny O's Christmas angels on the fancy tree, and we have Gramps' childhood ornaments on our family tree. How special is that?"

Reese had already picked up several of the ornaments to study them. "Great Grandmother O'Hara was some fine artist. Look at these, Mama."

"I know. I've already looked at them. Each one of them seems to tell a story about what was going on in their lives at the time. I think you have her artist genes." Jillian searched the box for the ornament with the doves. "This is my favorite—the one I showed to you before. It makes me feel closer to your grandparents to think about the oak tree out back, and how your gramps and his mother could hear the doves cooing just like we do. I can imagine with Gramps' father away at sea so much, she thought of herself and Gramps just like the two doves on the limb, alone and huddled together. And you know how he loved sitting out there on the balcony watching the sea and listening to the birds."

She turned to Stuart. "We never talked again about giving the carriage house apartment a name. I really like the sound of Dove's Landing." She waited for a response. "Do you like it?"

There was a moment of silence—almost a holy silence—before Stuart answered. "Dove's Landing. I do like it. I think it's perfect."

Jillian sighed. "Great. But everyone gets a vote. Raise your right hand for yes, boys." All hands went up. "What do you say we finish decorating the tree with these family treasures? And just maybe you can come up with some stories of your own. That's a special way we can remember Gramps this Christmas, his first Christmas in heaven."

Chapter Nine

---◆---

Thursday, December 18
Jacksonville

The car sputtered as Anna Beth turned into the parking lot at the Jacksonville Beach Golf Club. She parked under an oak tree, lowered the driver's-side window a couple of inches for fresh, cool air, and turned to look at her sleeping baby in the car seat. As she waited, she thought how grateful she was that her baby knew nothing of her distress and could sleep so peacefully.

The sunset was beginning to flush the skies with brilliant coral, and Anna Beth looked out over the marsh grasses, the palm trees, the lush fairway grass, and the reflection of the late-afternoon clouds in the meandering streams of water that snaked through the course. The shimmering beauty giving her a brief respite from her stormy life, she gazed and inhaled the peaceful views as one who was memorizing the scene with the expectation of not seeing it again for a very long time.

Alicia's slamming of the passenger-side door jolted Anna Beth from her mesmerized state. "Oh, I'm sorry. I should have been quieter. I see Johanna is asleep."

"It's okay. She sleeps soundly. How was work?"

"It's work. Trying to make some money during the holidays before next semester's classes start again. The manager wants me to continue to work here part time and go to school, but I don't know. Tips are good, so I can't complain." Alicia took off her shoes and rubbed her socked feet. "If anything, this job has taught me I don't want to do this kind of work the rest of my life. Flipping burgers and serving drinks make my dream of teaching kindergarten seem like a vacation. I'm glad you called, and thanks for giving me a ride home."

"You're welcome, and I'm glad your dreams will be coming true. I remember having dreams." A melancholy Anna Beth stared into the distance. "I'm sorry we haven't been able to see much of each other the last couple of months. You're living at home and going to college, and my life is so different now after I had to give up the apartment. Living with Miss Edith, still working at the supermarket part time, and taking care of Johanna. I've really missed you. But . . ." She hesitated. "There's another reason I wanted to see you today."

"Oh? What's up?"

"I came to say goodbye." Seeing Alicia's confused expression, she hurried on. "I'm leaving Jacksonville. I can't keep living like this: working only part time because there's no one to take care of my baby, and not being able to provide for Johanna like she needs because I'm only working part time. And then I feel like I'm freeloading on Miss Edith. She won't let me pay her anything." She shook her head. "I just have to make a change. It's time."

Alicia's confusion had moved to dismay. "But Miss

Edith said—"

Anna Beth interrupted. "I know she says I can stay with them as long as I need to, but it's not right. I moved in two months ago when I gave up my apartment. The rent money I saved helped me take care of Johanna. But like I said—it's just not right. I need to move on, get a new job, and I'm hoping my mom will at least help me get a better-paying job." Her lip quivered, and then she started to cry quietly. "It's just so hard, Alicia. If I don't have a good job, I don't have money to give Johanna the things she needs and some things I want her to have. But if I have a good job, half my money goes for childcare, and I'm not there when Johanna needs me. There just seems to be no answer. My daughter deserves better than me and better than I can give her."

"I'm sorry, Anna Beth. I wish I had a magic wand or some fairy dust or something to make things better for you and your baby. Is all the money from John gone?"

"Gone. Mom's been no help with rent or my living expenses since she left months ago, and then I had some medical bills that were my responsibility. That's why I moved in with Miss Edith. I have just enough money to get me to Hilton Head. Beyond that, I don't know." Anna Beth took the steering wheel in both hands as though it would pilot her back on course. Then she silently lowered her head to the wheel. "I don't know what else to do, Alicia. I just don't know."

Alicia cleared her throat. "Anna Beth, I'm about to ask you a serious question. I don't want to upset you, but I have to ask."

"What?"

"Have you ever thought of giving Johanna up for adoption?" Her friend waited.

Anna Beth had no response.

Alicia continued to plead her case. "It could be the best

thing for you and for Johanna. You could get a part-time job and go to nursing school. That's all you've ever wanted to be. You could still be a nurse. And think of how many couples really want a baby, and they especially want an infant. Johanna's only a little over two months old. She would have good parents and a good home. And you're young, Anna Beth. You can have dreams again."

Anna Beth remained silent, waiting for more questions. When Alicia said no more, she responded. "I've heard all this from Miss Edith. She thinks adoption would be best, too, for Johanna and me, but I can't give Johanna away. And dreams? You say I can have dreams again. If I gave her up, all my dreams would be of her. I would constantly be looking for her in every girl's face I saw for the rest of my life. I love her so much. She's my daughter. And what would John think if I gave her up?"

"I can't really tell you what John would think, but I know he really loved you, and I can imagine he would want what's best for you and for Johanna. And in a perfect world, you could keep Johanna, love her like crazy, and go to nursing school. Then you two could have a good life together. But . . . you don't live in a perfect world, Anna Beth."

"Perfect? I'd settle for a lot less than that if I could be the best mother I can be for Johanna."

"Maybe that means loving her enough to allow her a good life with a family that would love her and do good things for her."

Anna Beth sobbed. "I don't know what to do. I just feel like I'm walking through a minefield, and the next step could be my last. I can't turn around and go back, and I don't know how to move forward." She wiped her eyes on her jacket sleeve and turned when she heard Johanna crying. She got out of the car, got her baby, and returned to the driver's seat. "Can you reach back there and get her bottle out of the bag?"

Alicia got the bottle and handed it to Anna Beth. "It's warm."

"Yes, it must be a bit warm for her."

"Could I hold her and feed her?"

"Sure." Anna Beth carefully placed her daughter in Alicia's outstretched arm, wondering if this might be the last time Alicia would ever hold Johanna.

For several moments, they sat quietly with only sweet baby sounds and the sea breezes. Anna Beth watched as Alicia cuddled Johanna and smiled.

Could I ever give Johanna up? Could I bear knowing someone else was feeding my daughter and enjoying her milk breath and feeling her warmth?

She waited until the bottle was almost empty before taking Johanna back.

"I should get you home, and I need to get back to Miss Edith's to finish packing. Nothing left but our clothes and a few personal items. To pay bills, I had to sell what furniture I had. I don't imagine Mom will be thrilled about that."

"When are you leaving?"

"I'm planning to leave early in the morning and stay with my mom and Rodney for Christmas. Maybe something will change when she sees Johanna." She took the bottle from the baby's puckered lips. "After all, who couldn't fall in love with this little bundle? I'm so glad she has John's dark hair and eyes. I know he would have loved her, really loved her."

"Are you saying your mom still hasn't seen her?"

"That's what I'm saying. If it hadn't been for you and Miss Edith, I don't know what I would have done when she was born. But maybe when Mom sees her, she'll change her mind."

"Does she even know you're coming to Hilton Head?"

"Sort of. She thinks I'm just coming for Christmas. She doesn't know that I'm coming tomorrow prepared to stay, and that I need her help in getting a job."

"Do you think it's good to spring this on your mom when you get there? The part about your coming to stay? You know how she reacts to things."

"Probably not a good idea. Maybe I'll give her a call tomorrow when I'm on the road."

Anna Beth dropped Alicia off at her house. They embraced and promised to stay in touch.

Alicia opened the door to the back seat, leaned in, and gave Johanna a kiss. "Goodbye, sweet baby. I know one way or another, your mother will do what is best for you and for herself." She backed out of the car, gently closed the door, and took Anna Beths's hand. "We'll be friends no matter what, but just think about what I said."

Anna Beth nodded in agreement. "Do you remember why I named her Johanna?"

"Sure. Her name is from your name and John's name."

"That's what I thought, too, but Miss Edith looked it up. *Johanna* means "God is gracious." I sure wish He was."

Anna Beth closed the door, took the driver's seat, and waved goodbye.

———.———

Friday morning, December 18
Jacksonville

It was a cloudy and unusually cool morning for December. She could only hope the rain would hold off until she got to Hilton Head. It was less than a three-hour drive, but it seemed a million miles away, and it would take her longer with stops for the baby.

Anna Beth took the last two boxes from Mr. Harry and put them into the trunk of her car. He joined Miss Edith, who stood on the steps of the back porch. She was holding tightly to the baby. Anna Beth got in and started the car. She wanted it to be warm for Johanna.

She approached Miss Edith and Mr. Harry. "I can't thank you all enough for all you've done for me. Maybe one day, I can find a way to repay you."

Miss Edith handed the baby to her. "We didn't do a solitary thing expecting repayment, girl. We loved John, and we all lost him. And we have loved you and that baby girl of yours. You brought some life into this house. We're gonna miss you. I hope you know you can always come back."

Anna Beth pulled the blanket from Johanna's face. "I thank you for that too. And I'll make sure Johanna knows all about you and about her daddy."

Anna Beth's eyes brimmed with tears. Miss Edith came down the steps and walked her to the car. Anna Beth put the baby in the car seat and turned to embrace Miss Edith. "I don't know what's going to happen, but I'll call you. Don't worry about me, okay? Things have to get better, and I'll do whatever it takes to make things right for my daughter."

"Just think about the things I told you. You can't change the past, Anna Beth, but you can make choices now that would change your future. You're young, and you know that Harry and I will be praying for you. For your safety, for your peace of mind, and for you to have a good life. I know with what you've been through, it's hard to think that God is gracious, but He is. This Christmas season is all about that. And all you have to do is to look into that baby's face and remember what you named her, you hear?"

"Yes, ma'am. I won't forget." She kissed Miss Edith's cheek.

Miss Edith reached into her apron pocket for something and slipped it into Anna Beth's hand. "It's not much. Just consider it your Christmas present."

Anna Beth opened her palm to reveal a hundred-dollar bill. "Oh, you don't need to do this. Mr. Harry already bought me a full tank of gas to get me to Hilton Head."

"I don't *need* to do a thing but breathe. I *want* to do this. Take it."

"Thank you so much. This will be a big help." She hugged Miss Edith for the last time and started to walk away. After a few steps, she turned around. "You know, Miss Edith, you're the closest thing to a real mother I ever had. I mean, the kind of mother Johanna deserves."

Anna Beth got in the car and pulled out of the driveway. She knew she was leaving the only safe harbor she had ever experienced, and she could not know what was ahead of her.

She drove for about an hour until she was safely out of morning traffic. This stretch of I-95 would be a parking lot next week with folks traveling for Christmas. She looked at the clock on the dashboard. Nine thirty. It was time—time to make the dreaded call to her mom. Calling her mom while she was at work might keep her from blowing her stack.

Anna Beth had seen a sign for a rest area coming up—a place she could pull over for this conversation. She turned into the stop and parked near the restroom facility. Johanna was sound asleep, so Anna Beth took a deep breath and dialed her mom's number.

Gina answered on the second ring. "Hello." Her voice was weak and gruff.

"Hi, Mom. It's Anna Beth."

"Hi, Sugar Pie." That was all.

"I thought I'd call you and tell you I'm on my way to Hilton Head. I decided to come a few days early to avoid the Christmas traffic." She waited.

"You're coming today?"

"Yes, ma'am. I should be there by noon if this car holds out. You gave me your address last week when I told you I was coming. I know you're probably at work, and maybe I should have called you yesterday." Anna Beth paused.

Her mom was glum. "Not a good time, and it wouldn't have mattered if you called yesterday."

Anna Beth recognized this numbness in her mom's voice. She was either hungover or bummed out about something.

"Did I call at a bad time? Are you at work?"

"I'm home. Called in sick today. So you'd better find someplace else to stay."

Anna Beth felt that familiar grip in her stomach when she had to deal with her mom. "But Mom, I was hoping I could be there for Christmas and that maybe I could stay on a while. You said one time you could get me a good job."

"Things change, Anna Beth."

"I know." Anna Beth's life had been a steady cycle of changes. "Are you and Rodney having trouble?"

"You might call it that, but we're just having a rough spell. You know everybody has a rough spell now and then. But things won't get better if you're around, especially with a kid."

"Her name is Johanna, Mom." Anna Beth's mind froze. The minefield. She couldn't turn around and go back, and she didn't know what she was walking into. "You're saying you don't want me to come, and you don't want to see your granddaughter?"

"Sugar Pie, you don't have to make it sound like that. It's just that we don't have room, and we're running low on money. Things aren't good like they were before. But I know they'll get better. Now's just not a good time. And like I told you when you decided to have that kid, you made your bed and you gotta lie in it. I told you straight up not to count on me."

"You've never even seen her, Mom."

Before her mother could even reply, Anna Beth closed her phone, dropped it into the passenger's seat, and leaned her head back.

What is wrong with me? Why did I ever think this might work? I knew better. This is everything I don't want for Johanna. But now what? I have no good choices. No good options. None.

She sat a moment, the only sound Johanna's breathing as she slept. That and perhaps the sound of her own heart breaking.

God, please hear me. I don't know You very well, but Miss Edith says You're gracious. I don't even know what grace is, but it's got to be better than this. If You won't be gracious to me . . . I mean, You're God. You can be and do anything You want. Can't you at least be gracious to Johanna?

Tears fell from her cheeks, and her chest heaved from her fear and despair. She cried until there were no more tears, unaware of the passing time. The car, windows up, felt like a tomb—the tomb that now held the last bit of hope she had.

Johanna's cry roused Anna Beth. She took the baby from her car seat, held her close, and gave her a bottle. She looked into her daughter's little face, her long lashes almost sweeping her cheeks, the dark-brown swirls of curly hair. She wondered if her own mother had ever looked at her like this when she was a baby.

Dazed and unaware of time, she held her baby close and thought about what Miss Edith and Alicia had said. She knew she had no right to impose her situation on this innocent infant, but why would the best thing to do mean she would be eternally separated from her child, the one she loved more than life?

She didn't move a muscle until Johanna started to fret.

After a trip inside for a bathroom break and a diaper change, Anna Beth cranked the car. It sputtered. She turned the ignition again. More sputtering. She knew it wasn't cheap gas. Mr. Harry had filled up with the best for her yesterday. She got out and opened the hood as though she knew what she was looking at and could repair it.

In only a few moments an older gentleman walked to her side. "Having some car trouble this morning, young lady?"

Anna Beth was fearful but desperate, so she answered. "Yes, sir. It was running fine, but then when I tried to crank it, it started making a strange sound like sputtering."

He moved closer and leaned in to take a look. "Could be your spark plugs or something in the fuel line, or maybe you need a new filter." He took out his key and scraped it across the top of the spark plug. "Yep, these need replacing or cleaning for sure."

He stood up. "People are a lot like cars, you know. Sometimes we need a new spark or battery recharge, and sometimes it takes a complete overhaul to make things better. But for your car right now, I'm thinking new spark plugs will get the job done."

"Are they expensive?" Anna Beth was already counting the cost.

"Would be to some folks and wouldn't be to somebody else. Either way, it'll cost about a hundred dollars." He wiped the grime from his key with his thumbnail. "Try it now."

Anna Beth went to the driver's seat and turned the ignition. It sputtered like it really was wanting to crank. She tried again, and it started. She left the car running and got out to thank the man. "Sir, I'm really grateful. Could I pay you something?"

He let the hood of the car down and wiped his hands on his handkerchief. "No, ma'am. Nothing to pay me for because I didn't fix your problem. What I did was only temporary. You got some troubles that need a permanent fix, and there'll be somebody up ahead to help you with that." He rubbed his white beard. "You gotta be careful these days, ma'am. There are people and mechanics that'll take advantage of young ladies like you, but I know one who won't."

"You do? But do you think I can make it that far?"

"I do. Looks like you're headed north just like me. You'll be driving up on the outskirts of Bar Haven in about eighteen miles. You get off the freeway at the Bar Haven exit and drive into town. Stop at Griff's filling station right there on Seaside Drive on the right side. There's a sign, and it's painted white trimmed in green. If I know Griff, he'll have a big Christmas tree out front. It's the only station in town, so you can't miss it. Anyway, you stop there and be sure to ask for Griff, now, and tell him his old friend Josh sent you. He'll treat you right and fix what ought to be fixed, and he won't overcharge you."

"Yes, sir. I will do that. What about your last name?"

"Don't need one. Griff's my friend. He'll know."

"Thank you so much, sir, and I wish you a Merry Christmas."

A smile appeared in the middle of all his whiskers. "Merry Christmas to you, too, and to your little one in the back seat." He held his hand up as though waving. "And may the good Lord be gracious to you." He turned and walked away.

Anna Beth stood stunned. *Gracious. He said "May the good Lord be gracious" to me.*

Chapter Ten

———◆———

Friday, December 18
Bar Haven

A nna Beth took the exit to Bar Haven. Four miles on a road that took her straight to Seaside Drive, where she took a slight left turn. She almost smiled when she read the sign at the intersection: *BAR HAVEN—Where Everyone Counts.* She had spent the last half hour driving and lamenting that she'd never mattered to anyone except John and now Johanna, and maybe Miss Edith and Mr. Harry and Alicia.

How I'd like to be in a place where I counted. Really counted.

She slowed her driving to get a good look at a town where everyone counted.

Bar Haven was buzzing with holiday sights and sounds on this drizzly Friday afternoon. The sky was gray, but the quaint seaside town was aglow with Christmas. A canopy of red, yellow, blue, and green lights draped above and across

Seaside Drive as though suspended from heaven. Lampposts trimmed in greenery and red ribbons stood on every street corner. Shop windows were decked out in red and green. Even the hardware store had a set of red cookware in the window. And with a pair of binoculars, one could see the Christmas wreaths in the lighthouse windows out on the point. Everything in this town said *Noel*.

There were no traffic lights, only four-way stop signs at crossings, and she wasn't sure a traffic light could even be seen in this maze of Christmas lights. She drove slowly and looked for the filling station. Josh had said it would be on the right and the only one in town. She passed the church as she veered left. The town courthouse sat across the street.

There it was. The station stood a couple of blocks down. The gentleman named Josh had been right. The stark white station with painted green trim was not to be missed.

She drove into the lot and parked her car over to the side so as not to obstruct the gas pumps. Putting on her jacket, she wrapped Johanna warmly to protect her from the drizzle and unbuckled the car seat. She was wrestling with the umbrella and holding fast to the car seat when a teenage boy opened the glass door to the station. "Here, let me have your umbrella, ma'am. I'll take care of it for you."

"Thank you. I hope it didn't make a mess. I was just trying to keep my baby dry."

"No problem, ma'am. Lots worse messes made in here every day, but we know how to hose it down and clean it up. How can I help you? I'll tell you up front, we don't sell food and snacks in here, but we do have a public restroom."

"Thank you. Actually, I was looking for a man named Griff."

"You're in luck. He just got back from his coffee break, and he won't go to lunch before one o'clock. He likes them bear claws Miss Irma makes on Friday. He's out in the shop.

I'll go get him."

Anna Beth was relieved. With her trust issues, she'd doubted if what the stranger had told her was really true. So far so good.

She waited. The Christmas music was playing so loudly she had no doubt if her car windows had been down she would have heard it when she left the freeway.

In just a couple of minutes, a stout, balding man approached. He wore bright-green coveralls that matched the paint out front and had red shop rags stuck in all his pockets. "Beau, turn the music down for a few minutes, would you? I can't even hear myself think, let alone have a conversation with this customer." He looked at Anna Beth. "Sorry, ma'am. We do love our Christmas music. Beau starts it up the day after Thanksgiving, and it plays all day long except when the church bells play at ten in the morning and at three in the afternoon. We don't get many complaints, though. Something about Christmas music just makes us feel good. But you didn't come in here to find out what I think about Christmas music. How can I help you?"

"That's my car parked over there." Anna Beth looked out the window toward the car and nodded. "I think I need some new spark plugs. I left Jacksonville this morning on my way to Hilton Head, and when I stopped at the rest stop, my car wouldn't start again. It's been sputtering for a while. But a man there helped me and got my car started. I think he scraped off the spark plugs and told me to come to your station. And he said to tell you that Josh sent me."

Anna Beth eased when she saw the man's face break into a broad grin.

"Josh. So he's sent me another one. He's an old friend, and he's sent lots of customers my way through the years. I'll do my best to help you." He looked at the large wall clock fringed in Christmas lights. "It's nearly eleven o'clock.

No why don't you just take yourself and your little one across the street to Irma's?" He pointed to the café across the street. "Best place in town to eat, and she makes a chicken bog on Friday, one like you've never tasted. A bowl of that, a piece of her buttered cornbread, and a helping of sweet potatoes, and you'll think Christmas is already here. And if you get on over there, she might have a bear claw left. Nobody can cook like Irma. I'll get your car fixed up, and I'll send Beau over there to get you when it's ready."

Anna Beth took a breath. "Sir, I don't have very much money. Can you tell me what it'll cost to fix it?"

He nodded. "Well, ma'am. I can't rightly tell you until I take a look. But if Josh told you it's bad spark plugs, it probably is. He's usually right. It'll depend on how many need replacing. You got an older model, and it could take six. But you probably won't need all six, so I would think a hundred dollars ought to do it. I'll send Beau to tell you how much it'll be."

"Thank you. I'll just get my umbrella and go over to the cafe." Anna Beth handed him the keys. "The car is packed with all our Christmas things, so I hope you'll be careful."

"Yes, ma'am. As careful as if that's all you had in this world."

If he only knew that a few boxes and Johanna are *all I have in this world.* "Thank you, sir."

"You're mighty welcome. Now you just take your baby and go have yourself some lunch, and Irma won't mind if you want to stay there for a while 'til I've finished up. You'll be warm and out of the rain. She usually takes a liking to babies. You just tell her that ol' Griff sent you over there."

Anna Beth walked to the corner to cross the street. She was amazed that cars actually stopped to allow her to cross. She entered the café and was greeted by a middle-aged waitress.

"Mr. Griff across the street sent me over here. He thinks you have the best food in town."

A rather large woman dressed in a colorful muumuu with her hair in a bright-green turban came from behind the counter. "Well, shugah, if Griff sent you, you get the best seat in the house. You just follow Irma."

Anna Beth followed her to the corner booth, put the baby's car seat in the corner, and slid in beside her.

"You can see the practically the whole town from here. And if you squinch your eyes, you can see the lighthouse out there on the point. And besides, it'll be quiet back here for the baby to nap. And you, too, if you need a nap. No use bringing you a menu. Today's the day I cook my famous Geechee chicken bog—one that'll stick to your skinny little ribs."

Anna Beth adjusted the car seat to face her and took Johanna in her arms. "Yes, ma'am. I've never had it, but I'm sure if you make it, it's good."

"I'm no braggart, but I'm a Geechee gal who knows how to cook, taught by Mama and my grandmama. And I'm telling you, you don't need a silver fork to eat good food. Won't find a silver fork around here, but I'll have your plate out before you can get that blanket off the baby. I wanna see that pretty little thing."

"I think I'd also like one of those bear claws that Mr. Griff told me about. I'll just take that in a bag if you don't mind. Sounds like a tasty afternoon snack for the road."

"Comin' yo' way."

———•———

Anna Beth enjoyed her lunch and her conversation. Miss Irma held the baby until customers started arriving. "Well, shugah, nothing would please me more than to sit right here with you and this bundle of love all afternoon, but my job's feeding hungry people, and there's about to be a stampede. Chicken bog always brings them in."

Anna Beth almost smiled. "Yes, ma'am. I know why they're coming." She looked at her empty bowl. Not one grain of rice or crumb of cornbread remained, and there were only streaks of the glaze that had covered the sweet potatoes. She couldn't remember when she had eaten such a tasty meal.

She had the corner to herself. Miss Irma was right. She could see the whole town, and she could see everyone who entered the café. No doubt they were all regular customers, and they all knew each other. She didn't think of herself as eavesdropping, but she heard conversations about the Christmas sale at the local mercantile and last night's Christmas parade down Seaside Drive and the celebrations planned for the weekend. She heard talk of costumes and a live nativity Sunday night. She had already noticed the flyer in the window and had read it backward since the flyer was facing the street.

If only I could have grown up in a town like this, a real community where people know each other, where everyone knows Miss Irma cooks chicken bog on Fridays, and where everybody matters.

She pulled her map from her bag and unfolded it. Savannah was about an hour away and Hilton Head almost an hour beyond that.

Why am I even looking at Hilton Head? If I get there, where will I stay? Maybe I should turn around and go back to Miss Edith's. She said I could. If I really counted to somebody, I wouldn't be sitting here wondering what to do, trying to make life decisions for Johanna and myself all by myself. She sighed. *I just wish I knew what to do.*

The lunch crowd soon disappeared, and the noise and

chatter went out the door with them. She had fed Johanna, who was now sleeping. She leaned her head back against the booth, but sleep wouldn't come for her. Only questions and options. She needed answers and direction.

After a while, Mr. Griff came through the door and spied her in the corner. He slid into the seat across from her. Two cups of fresh coffee appeared on the table as he started to speak. "Well, little lady, I have news, and I decided to deliver it myself rather than send Beau. Some of it's good, and some of it's not so good."

Anna Beth felt the heaviness return. "Yes, sir. I think I'd rather hear the good news first."

"It's the spark plugs, just like Josh said. But you need four, and you need a new fuel filter. The cost'll be about what I said it would be. And that should have your car humming for a while."

"That is good news. But what about the bad news?"

"Well, it's only bad if you have somewhere you need to be this evening, because I only have one plug that'll work in that '95 Ford Taurus you drive. Now, I called, and they have some at the parts store in Savannah, and I'm sending Beau to get them, but he won't be back in time to get your car fixed today. So, I hope you didn't need to get somewhere by nightfall."

She wished she knew where that somewhere might be. "But that's so much trouble for you, sir."

"Not really. I try to keep a few parts on hand, and when I looked around, I realized I'm running real low on some standard parts. I made a list for Beau. He's supposed to be keeping up with my inventory, but he's better at cleaning windshields and working the cash register. And honestly, it'll take him longer than most to get to Savannah and back today."

"I see. I understand about inventory. I had a job in a

supermarket, and I helped with that, and it's not always easy to predict what you'll need."

"That's for sure. Maybe I need to hire you." He smiled. "I just came to tell you like I said I would. I'll just keep your car parked in the locked garage tonight so your Christmas things'll be safe. And if you give me your name and number, I'll call in the morning when it's ready. There's a bed-and-breakfast a couple of blocks down the street. I'm sure they'll put you up for the night, and they'll treat you right."

Anna Beth was almost panicked. She barely had enough money to pay for the car repair. There was no money for an overnight stay. "Sir, if it's not too much trouble, I think I'll just come get my car and bring it back to you in the morning." She paused. "But tomorrow's Saturday. Are you open on Saturday?"

"Oh yes, but we don't work on the Lord's Day, so I'll have your car running before Sunday. You can take your car, but I can't guarantee you that it'll crank for you in the morning. Let me go do a little more scraping and cleaning. That might help get you started in the morning."

Anna Beth thought she felt Griff's eyes peering into her thoughts. "I promise, sir, that I'll bring it back. I know you're getting the parts, so I'm not skipping town. I just need so much that's in my car. Babies require a lot, you know. I think I'd rather have it close by."

"Not worried one bit about that. By the way, what's your name?"

"I'm sorry. I should have told you." She searched her bag for a pen and paper. "My name's Anna Beth Nelson, and here's my cell number. I'll just wait for you to call in the morning, and I'll bring it right in."

"Sounds good. Give me a while to get your car off the rack. This job gave me something to do today, or else I'd just have had to listen to Beau and clean up the mess I made yesterday. Irma won't mind a bit if you stay here a little longer out of the drizzle where it's warm. I'll call you when it's ready for you to pick it up. It'll take me a little longer than usual since Beau's going to Savannah, and I'll be pumping gas and working the register."

Griff slid out of the booth, stuck the scrap of paper in his coverall pocket, and walked to the counter. He pulled out his wallet and laid some bills for his coffee on the counter. She watched as he leaned over the counter and said something to Irma. She saw Irma's nod and smile and guessed they were old friends.

Anna Beth sat patiently for another hour before Griff called. Irma had not brought her ticket, and she wasn't about to raise her hand as though she expected more service. Enough kindness had already been extended to her. She wrapped the blanket tightly around Johanna and slid out of the seat, pulled the car seat out behind her, and walked to the counter to pay for her lunch. She tapped on the bell to get someone's attention.

Irma was in the kitchen cleaning the counters, but her reedy, strong voice could be heard through the empty café as she sang "I'll Be Home for Christmas." She appeared, her hips swaying to the soulful tune.

"You have a beautiful voice, Miss Irma. I like the song you were singing."

"Just warming up. I'll be singing this Sunday evening at our first live nativity over at the church. We're having a real manger with folks dressed up in costumes, special lighting, and bells playing, and seems like I even heard something about life-sized animals. Why, this is the best weekend of the whole year in Bar Haven. People come from all around for our Christmas programs. Too bad you'll miss it. You need something else, shugah?"

"Just my check, please, ma'am."

Irma shuffled through the tickets on the counter. "I declare, I can't seem to find it. If it's not here, that must mean it's all been taken care of."

"But—"

"Ain't no butts around here but mine. Besides it's Christmas, and I do hope you'll come back to see me sometime." Irma reached under the counter and pulled out a box. "Here's that bear claw you wanted."

"I'd really like to pay you for my meal, but thank you, ma'am, so much. I really enjoyed the chicken bog and sweet potatoes. I'll be learning how to make that."

"You come on back anytime. Irma'll be glad to teach you, but she may not tell you all her secrets." Irma winked. "Now you go have yourself a Merry Christmas, you hear?"

———•———

Anna Beth was glad the rain had stopped. She asked Griff for permission to leave her car parked at the station while she strolled through town. She passed by Martha's Garden B&B that Griff had suggested but decided to call for rates rather than going in. While there was a sign in the window advertising a Christmas Special for $185 for two nights, the clerk who answered reported their last room had been booked for over a week with out-of-towners coming in for the Christmas events in Bar Haven.

It didn't matter. Anna Beth had only the hundred-dollar bill Miss Edith gave her and another ninety dollars to her name. She had to pay for car repairs, and Johanna would need diapers and formula before she got something figured out. It wouldn't be the first night she had spent in a car, but it was the first where she was supposed to be the adult. She was just grateful the rain and the wind had subsided and the temperatures were not frigid.

She purchased bottled water and some snacks that would get her through the night, then thought of options of where to park for the night. It needed to be a safe place, a place where she wouldn't be noticed.

I could park at the lighthouse out on the point, but then how would I explain why I was there if my car won't crank in the morning? I can't park at Griff's station or on Seaside Drive because anyone driving through town would see me. The church? Maybe there's a parking lot in the back. It's in town and only a few blocks from the station. Surely a church parking lot would be a safe place, and no one would be there on a Friday night.

Waiting until after dark and until Griff's station was closed, she returned to her car. She was still confused but at least settled about her decision for parking for the night. She had water and snacks and clothing and blankets to stay warm. She unlocked the back seat and secured Johanna in the car seat and sat next to her to change her diaper and give her a bottle.

When Johanna was sleeping soundly, Anna Beth started the car and drove back up the street to the church and turned into the parking lot. She drove around to the back near the trees, parked where she could see anyone entering, and turned the car off. She reached for Irma's box with the bear claw. When she opened it, she found a muffin, a peanut butter and jelly sandwich made with Irma's cornbread, an apple, and a bear claw, napkins, and a bottle of water. She smiled at the thought.

When she went to put the box down, she saw a four-inch block of wood painted white and trimmed in green, with a key ring and key on the end of it. Painted in primitive letters on the side, it read *Restroom.*

Maybe God was gracious after all.

Chapter Eleven

---◆---

Saturday morning, December 20
Bar Haven

After an early-morning hot breakfast and a quick load of the truck, Reese closed the tailgate and climbed into the passenger's seat with his duffle bag. His dad had already cranked the truck. Stuart said, "Sorry Riley's not happy, but with yesterday's rain, we must get all the work done today, and that means no time to deal with his shenanigans. Got plenty of help, and we should have things looking like Bethlehem by early afternoon."

As they backed out of the driveway, Reese saw Riley standing at the back door, looking like a sad-eyed puppy. He'd caused a bit of a ruckus this morning when he heard he couldn't go with them. "He'll get over it. But maybe when we're almost done, you could come back and get him and let him spread the hay or something to make him feel like he helped."

"That's a good idea. By the way, did you leave some

room in the back for some sandbags? Zack and his sons went to the coast yesterday and packed wet sand in bags. I told him I'd come pick them up. Supposed to be clear but windy tomorrow, and Buck suggested sandbags to weigh down the support frames for your animals. We don't need a camel with two humps taking a nosedive into the crowd."

"That's for sure, Dad. We may need to set up the animals first and pick up the sandbags later." Reese was proud of his work and he didn't want it sandbagged before anyone saw it. When Mrs. Franklin had told him the live nativity was a new tradition and the painted animals would be used for years to come, he'd been even more proud and cautious. "You could get Riley to help you. That'll make him happy."

They pulled into the parking lot on the south side of the church where the manger was. They were the first ones there. His dad was always the first one to arrive. Tardiness was a serious vice in his dad's eyes.

Reese was surprised when he spied a slow-moving car at the far corner of the parking lot and saw the driver as the car passed them. The driver was a blond lady, and one he didn't recognize. He wondered what a stranger would be doing in the church parking lot on a Saturday morning.

Within fifteen minutes, a team of men and teenage boys was busy. Some were wiring and hanging the star that looked more like a disco ball. Some were covering the chicken wire on top with palmetto branches and sawgrass. Others spread hay and Spanish moss on the ground in the crèche and around the outside where the wooden animals would be placed. In only a couple of hours, the scene had been transformed. Buck, with Reese beside him, placed the animals according to the sketches Reese had made. The final touch was the two doves perched atop the frame.

Then a team of men and boys hauled about thirty chairs out of the church and placed them at an angle from the structure. Buck looked at the scene. "That should do it, boys. The program itself lasts less than an hour, and most folks can stand that long. Besides, I hear some singing is involved. Set up like this, the chairs won't be in the way for the ones who just drive by to see." He sidled up to Reese and whispered. "Not sure they have Spanish moss in Bethlehem, but that frame's dripping in it. Tried to tell those boys to wear their jackets and put on some gloves or else they'll be scratching tonight. Chiggers."

Reese laughed. "Yes, sir. I learned that lesson a while back." He gestured. "Dad went to get Riley and the sandbags. Said he'd be back in about twenty minutes."

"Good deal. The sandbags will keep our work standing, even in the gusty winds." The other men were loading up their tools and ladders when Buck put his hand on Reese's shoulder. "Come on, son. One last thing—the most important thing and what all this is about. You can help me get the manger. And I built a stool for Mother Mary. We can't let her stand up for three hours. I think she deserves to sit just like she was in your sketch. And besides, I want to get it set up while there's still some fresh hay. No Spanish moss in the manger. Don't want to douse Baby Jesus in vinegar to keep the chiggers away."

Reese heard his dad's horn as he entered the parking lot. That was a new thing Riley had been getting him to do whenever they pulled into the driveway at home.

Riley got out of the truck and headed straight for Reese. "Your animals look good. I mean they look real, Reese."

"Thanks, little brother. We saved a special job for you. You see the manger under there?"

"Yep."

"And that small pile of hay over there next to the tree."

"Yep."

"Your job is to put that hay in the manger. Make sure it

has no Spanish moss, and make it nice and soft like a nest, just like the duck's nest we saw with the eggs in it. If you don't have gloves, you can borrow mine."

"I can do that." Riley held up his bare hands to Reese.

Reese handed him his gloves and watched Riley run toward the hay as though it might disappear before he got there. Then he joined his dad and Buck to haul the sandbags and place them strategically on the wooden braces to support the animals.

Buck backed away with the last bag in place. "I think that'll do it, boys. That camel and that donkey won't be going anywhere. They were the ones to worry about, but no more. And we don't have to worry about Monday-morning headlines: 'Pastor's Wife Injured by Flying Donkey.'" They laughed. "And having it all set up for church tomorrow ought to generate some excitement—as if we needed any more excitement about Christmas around here. Good job, everyone!" Buck announced.

Riley ran back to Reese as fast as he'd run to the hay. "I did it, Reese. Baby Jesus will have a soft bed. I hope somebody brings him a blanket."

"That's good. Tell Mama about the blanket." He lifted the duffle bag he was holding. "Mr. Buck. I have my paints right here if you think anything needs touching up."

"I think everything's just fine, son. By the way, how are you coming on your mom's doves?"

Riley got his wide-eyed look and grabbed Reese's arm. "That's a secret 'til Christmas. We promised not to tell."

"It's okay. Mr. Buck cut out the doves for the nativity, and he cut out the two I'm painting for Mama."

"But does he know about the sign we made?"

"He does now."

Buck asked, "Sign?"

"Yes, sir. She doesn't know about the doves I'm making,

but Mama wants to name the carriage house apartment Dove's Landing. So, Riley and I found an old scuffed-up board in the storage shed. We cleaned it up, and Dad helped us sand it down so I could paint the letters on it. So now the sign has the two doves perched together on a small limb that Dad attached to board. I hope to finish the lettering this afternoon."

Buck nodded. "Now that's a Christmas present. A special one your mama won't forget. Symbols of peace over your grandfather's door would make him mighty proud too."

"I really appreciate your help, Mr. Buck. I can paint them, but no way could I have cut them out like you did. I'll be sure to tell Mama you really helped out."

Riley piped up. "And I did too."

Buck pointed to the nativity. "And look what happens when we all pitch in, lend a hand, and help out. Jesus shows up for sure."

———·———

Anna Beth had been awake for a while with her thoughts as little Johanna slept. She had been surprised by the trucks showing up at the church so early. It startled her that she might have lost track of her days and wondered if it was already Sunday. Never had she been more grateful that her car cranked on the first turn of her key.

She drove through town toward Griff's station. Nothing open yet. Griff's station wasn't open for another twenty minutes, but the door to the restroom was there on the side of the building next to the garage. She parked, used the key she'd found in the car last night, and took Johanna inside to get cleaned up and ready for the day. She had a plan. She would feed Johanna, get coffee at the convenience store down the street, and eat the muffin Irma had packed for her. Then she would walk down to the library. She needed information.

She was sitting in her car by the time Griff showed up. She got out and handed him the key. "I found this in my car. I think it must belong to you, sir."

"Well, I'll be. I would have been looking for that this morning. Thank you." He smiled a knowing smile, a kind smile. "I'll get right on fixing your car this morning. Irma will open up here in a few minutes."

"Thanks, but I have some other plans. Maybe I'll see Irma for lunch. I saw that you have a library down the street. I think I'll take Johanna for a nice walk in the morning sunshine, and we'll visit the library." She didn't tell him that she needed information and that she had spent a good portion of the night thinking, even talking out loud to herself, trying to decide what to do.

Her science teachers had taught her about the scientific method: define your question; gather data; formulate a hypothesis; and try to make some predictions. She knew what the question was, but to come up with predictions and a plan, she needed one critical piece of information. Her decision was made, but how she carried it out was based solely on that one piece of information.

Griff nodded. "Better enjoy the sunshine. My wife told me it's supposed to get colder this evening, and these nice ocean breezes we're enjoying today are going to be blowing cold in the morning, like they're mad with us."

"Yes, sir. I will." She took Johanna out of her car seat and put her in the baby sling to keep her close. She decided to carry the car seat with her.

"I should be done in an hour. I won't call you. I know that librarian, and she's one fine lady until somebody makes a sound in her library. I'm not sure what she'd do if a phone rang. You just take your time. I'll be here when you get back."

She walked the few blocks and got a cup of coffee. Johanna had been fed and was sleeping soundly, so Anna Beth found the nearest street bench, ate her muffin, and drank her coffee. She had been in town less than twenty-four hours, but she knew where things were and she felt comfortable here. And being so near the ocean was another gift this town offered. The residents knew each other and cared about each other. She had learned that sitting in the café yesterday as she heard their conversations.

She was drinking the last sip when she heard the music from Griff's station. It filled the town and was audible all the way to the library. She climbed the steps to the glass doors. The young girl who sat at the front desk and offered help did not look like the librarian Griff had described. She was relieved. Anna Beth inquired about internet service. She was also secretly hoping for a plug to recharge her cellphone. The girl simply said, "Follow me."

Observing the girl's somewhat mechanical body language, Anna Beth followed her to a room with several computer stations. There was no one in the room. Anna Beth asked softly. "Is there a charge based on time, or do I need a code?"

Holding herself stiffly, the girl spoke in a faint monotone, but she was kind. "It is free if you have a library card, but I do not think I have ever seen you before, which means you probably do not have a card. So technically, there should be a charge." She paused, then nodded. "But it is Christmas, so I will give you the code. We are not busy today. Stay as long as you like. We close early this afternoon at four o'clock." The girl logged onto the computer, put in the code, and said before she left the room, "If I can be of any further help, I'll be at the front desk."

Anna Beth thanked her, removed Johanna from the baby sling, and put her in the car seat on the floor next to her. She typed in her queries. With each question, she obtained a bit more information. She stayed at the library until almost one o'clock. It was quiet, warm, and safe with bathroom facilities. With no one else in the room, she was free to feed Johanna.

She clearly had her answers. The state of Georgia did have a Safe Haven law that allowed mothers to leave their infant babies with a staff person or a volunteer at a fire station, a medical facility, or a police station without identifying herself. No questions asked. But the infant could be no older than thirty days. Although Johanna was small because she'd been born early, she was two months old. Leaving her at the local hospital would have been the safest and best option. Johanna would have been cared for by professionals until someone adopted her, someone kind like Griff or Irma, and someone who lived in a town where everyone counted. Johanna could have had a good life here, better than the life Anna Beth could offer her.

But information had eliminated her best option—she could not leave Johanna under the Safe Haven law. She was almost relieved. She had spent most of the night trying to imagine leaving her baby in the hands of a stranger.

Then came the onerous cloud of questions about the future, the most immediate being where would she spend tonight and what would she do when her money ran out.

Chapter Twelve

---◆---

Saturday afternoon

Reese was out in the carriage-house garage finishing the lettering on the sign. He'd made sure his mama was busy, and he had Riley on guard in case she came out to check on them. Giving his curious little brother something to do kept him away from the paint.

Reese always studied the subject before he painted. As he had done his research about the two-humped camel, he'd read about mourning doves to learn about their size, shape, habitat, nesting, coos, and colors. He made certain he chose the right paint colors: gray with black spots on the wings, a black bill, flesh-colored legs, and a ring of iridescent blue around the eyes. Male with slightly more vivid coloring, and female looked very similar, although the female dove's head was rounder. The distinction was subtle but could be seen in Reese's drawing and painting.

What a stroke of luck that his mama had found the Christmas ornament with the doves, and what timing. While he liked the thought of naming the carriage-house apartment, especially since Gramps had lived there for a while and he enjoyed the doves, Reese had not yet warmed up to the idea of someone else living in their backyard. But his mom's interest had given him the idea for her Christmas gift, and it was a reason to ask her to buy sunflower seeds and cracked corn to attract the doves. She did not hesitate.

After he read that doves like to eat from a tray or on the ground, he'd found an old wooden box in the shed and asked his dad to cut the sides down to make a tray. He filled it with the seeds and corn, raised his second-floor bedroom window a couple of inches, and secured the tray. It took a couple of days, but the birds, usually in pairs, began to come to the feeder. With the window raised, Reese could hear their coos early in the morning and sometimes in the late afternoon. He had read that some think the dove's coos are a call to seek peace. All Reese knew was that he liked the peaceful calls.

As the doves fed from the tray, he had opportunity to view them up close and memorize the colors. He mixed paint colors to get them just right and spent time on the feathers to give the birds a three-dimensional appearance. Now the wooden pair perched side by side on the small oak branch his father had secured to the sign.

Reese outlined the last three letters in the white paint and called Riley. "Come here, Riley. You want to paint the last three letters? All you have to do is to paint inside the lines." Having seen how Riley colored, Reese knew this move was chancy, but he knew it would mean something to his brother and to his mama that both her boys had worked on this project.

He pulled up a box for Riley to stand on. "You paint. I'll keep watch."

"Okay. I'll be careful, Reese. I'll do it good. I promise."

Only a few minutes passed and Riley said, "I'm done."

Riley's letters weren't perfect like his, but Reese wasn't going to change them. "Here, let me get that paint off you. How did you get it in your hair?" Reese started wiping it, only making it smear and get worse. Then he remembered the trick his dad had taught him about turpentine and paint. Rummaging for the can, he wet a rag and rubbed the paint off Riley's skin and out of his hair. "Now we got to get in and get you in the tub or else Mama will know we've been up to something."

Riley held his nose. "Puuweeh, that's stinky stuff. Okay, I'll go rub some dirt on me. When I'm real dirty, Mom sends me straight to get a bath. But we got to wrap the present."

"Can't wrap it until it's dry. Maybe tomorrow."

"Mama's really gonna like this. And I helped paint. You can teach me to paint, Reese. I know you can."

"Maybe another day. Mama'll be calling us for supper soon. Let me clean up this mess."

Reese put away his paints, washed his brushes, and put the sign in the spot where he'd been hiding it. Lucky for the boys, their mother was busy in the kitchen when they came inside and headed upstairs.

In another half hour both boys were back downstairs, wet hair but clean. Jillian was surprised. "You boys have already cleaned up before supper. Wow! You must think Santa's really taking notice. That's good. We're picking up burgers tonight."

"Why are we going for burgers?" Riley asked. "You been cooking."

"'*You've* been cooking,' Riley."

"Not me. I didn't cook."

Reese chuckled when his mama winked at him. "I was correcting your speech, Riley. It's *you've been cooking*, not *you been cooking*. Anyway, I *have* been cooking, preparing for Sunday lunch tomorrow. And guess what? We're eating in the dining room to practice for Christmas—ruby-red china, crystal goblets, and linen napkins. You boys were great at the Lamberts, but we need to practice one more time before our Christmas dinner. Your grandparents are coming from South Carolina, and guess who else is coming?"

Riley idled around her at the sink. "I don't know. Uncle Connor and Aunt Rose?"

"No, remember, Uncle Connor and his family are going to Florida to visit Aunt Rose's parents."

Reese tried next. "Pastor Franklin and Miss Rosemary."

"No, they're headed to North Georgia to see their son and his family. You're good guessers, but I'll tell you. The Lamberts are coming from Tybee Island. They don't have children, and when we invited them to celebrate with us, they were quick to say yes."

Riley joined Reese at the counter. "I'm the only children?"

"Yes, you're the only child."

"But what about Reese? He's a children."

"He counts as a young man. And that's why it's important that we practice our good manners one more time. There won't be a children's table since your cousins won't be here. I think you'll do just fine at the grownup's table." She wiped her hands. "Go tell your dad we're ready to go."

———•———

With the baby in the sling against her, Anna Beth left the computer room about one o'clock and thanked the silent girl at the front desk. She walked out of the library with her information. Unfortunately, what she had learned annihilated her one possible solution. She realized she was back to square one as she made the short walk to Griff's. She waved at him through the window. He came out to meet her. "Your car is finished, and it's in good shape. Should get you to wherever you want to go. I filled up your gas tank, and the whole bill came out to eighty dollars."

"That's so good, and I sure do appreciate it. Let me get to my purse."

"Like I said, it gave me something to do. Let's go inside. The wind's picking up." He opened the door for her and walked behind the counter where the cash register sat. "Will this be cash, check, or credit card?"

She put the baby carrier on the floor and reached into her purse "Cash." She had never had a credit card and had cleaned out her checking account.

Not expecting change back, especially since he'd filled her gas tank, she handed him the hundred-dollar bill Miss Edith had given her. But she was soon stuffing the twenty-dollar bill he handed her into her wallet. "I really appreciate your help, Mr. Griff. You're lucky to live in Bar Haven. I used to live in Georgia before my mom and I moved to Jacksonville when I was four or five. Jacksonville's a really big town. I think I'm more of a small-town girl. Bar Haven seems like a great place to raise children."

Griff came out from behind the counter with his hands in his coverall pockets. "You're mighty right. I'm glad the good Lord chose this place to be my home until I go Home." Griff's index finger pointed to the sky. "I'm fourth generation. I grew up in these marshlands, and my wife and I raised our two boys here." He rubbed his chin. "Oh, they went off to the big city for a while, but they're both back and raising their kids here."

"I can understand why."

Johanna whimpered, and Anna Beth cuddled her in the sling.

"Savannah's not far if you need some culture or want to go to a fancy restaurant. But for me, I get all the good eating I need at my table at home or at Irma's. Always plenty to do. Fishing, crabbing, and the weather's fairly mild. Except the cold wind's coming in today, but it won't last long."

"I was wondering about the lighthouse. How do I get there?"

"You just follow Seaside Drive out of town, and you'll come to a sign for Lighthouse Road. Take that right. It's just a few miles. Nobody out there. It's not active anymore. Hasn't been for years. Coast Guard put it up for sale a while back, and Old Man O'Hara bought it to preserve it. He passed away a while back, but I suppose his family still owns it and keeps it up. Good people around here."

"Yes, sir. And I would say you're one of them. I really appreciate your help. I should be on my way now. I need to get to the drugstore for a few items, and I may just take a drive out there to see the lighthouse and to sit while the sun's still shining." She turned and walked toward the door.

Griff followed her to the door and opened it. "It's been my pleasure to help you, Anna Beth. And if you ever come this way again, I hope you'll stop in. I know Irma would be glad to see you and that sweet little baby of yours. And if you decide to stay the night, the live nativity will be something real special tomorrow night. Whole town's talking about it."

"Thank you, sir, and Merry Christmas."

"And I hope you have a Merry Christmas and a bright new year."

Anna Beth drove to the convenience store, parked near-by, and went in for a loaf of bread and peanut butter. That would last her a few days. With the baby secure against her, she crossed the street to the drugstore and walked the aisles, putting only necessary items in her basket and counting her pennies with each. She found the card aisle and bought the least expensive box of stationery they had. Ordinarily, a box of pink stationery would have been a splurge, but it was a necessity for her new plan. Her desperation was fertile ground for new plans.

Shopping done, she drove in silence out to the light-house. She had grown weary of all the joyful Christmas music. It had done nothing good for her spirits, only reminding her that there were happy, joyful people with good lives in the world, and she wasn't one of them.

She parked near the lighthouse where she could look out to the ocean and moved the car seat with Johanna in it to the passenger's seat where she could see and easily tend to her. This would be their home for the night. Even in the car, she could already feel a change in the temperature. The wind was picking up, and the waves were capped with white as they lapped the shoreline. The marsh grasses fluttered. She took Johanna in her arms to make sure she was warm and to feed her. As the baby took the bottle, Anna Beth stared into the horizon where graying sky bled into colorless ocean. She thought of John, imagining what it had been like for him, living and working on an oil rig out of sight of land. And now his grave was the vast ocean.

She wondered how far one had to go to lose sight of land. She felt she was almost there, nothing to grasp or hold on to. She longed for John. She needed him, and Johanna needed him, but he was gone.

She stared into her baby's face. *How will you look when you're five? And twelve? And eighteen. I think you'll have your father's dark coloring and eyes and hair. But will you have his drive and energy, or will you be shy like me? Maybe you'll want to be a teacher or a doctor. I hope you'll want to be a mother.*

Anna Beth's tears dropped to her baby's face and ran off her puffy little cheek.

She didn't really know how to pray. She had only heard people pray when she started going to church with John. But she needed to talk to someone, and she had no one else. She could only hope God understood her as she didn't have the fancy words the church folks had. She begged, "Please, God, I have no one and nowhere to go, but I don't want that for Johanna. John really loved me and wanted to build a life with me, and working on that oil rig to give us a good future cost him his life. I know Miss Edith says that You love me, but I don't feel it. There's nothing in my life to make me know that. I want to believe it. Please let my tears be the only ones that ever touch my baby's cheeks. Please be gracious to her and provide somebody to love her as much as I do, somebody who can do for her and give her a real chance at life. Something I didn't have, and I can't give her. I'm not asking for anything for myself, God. Just be good to my little Johanna."

When Johanna was sleeping soundly, Anna Beth placed her in the car seat and wrapped her warmly. She reached in the back seat for the bag from the drugstore and removed the box of stationery. Daylight was slipping away, and this must be done. Using the box itself for a writing surface, Anna Beth began writing as neatly as she could. She wrote in spurts, at times staring out at the ocean as if the oncoming waves would bring the words she needed. When she had no more words, she read over the pages, folded them, and put them into two separate envelopes. That was finished, and now she had only the final thing to do.

Chapter Thirteen

---◆---

Sunday
Bar Haven

An unusually cold and rainy December had followed a mild hurricane season for the folks of Bar Haven. Chiseled into the flat, coastal landscape of Georgia, the town had little protection from the gale-like winds still blowing at midday on the Sunday before Christmas. The O'Haras came out of church holding tight to their hats and scarves. In all the rushing around, no one gave notice to the young woman in the brown trench coat next to the lamp post. That is, except Reese. He thought her to be the driver of the car he had seen in the church parking lot early Saturday morning.

Strands of her blond hair blew across her face, and she tried to tuck them into the gray hoodie she wore underneath her coat while she held tightly to the bundle covered in a red plaid wool blanket in her left arm. She walked past them as the O'Haras hurried to their car.

Reese watched her through the car window when she

started up the sidewalk to the front door of the church. She climbed the steps, gripped the brass doorknob . . . and then she turned around and walked away. Reese assumed the doors were already locked, as most people had left.

Stuart took a right turn out of the parking lot onto Second Avenue and asked, "So, Jillian, what's for lunch today?"

Before she could respond, Reese yelled, "Slow down, Dad. Wait, Dad. Stop."

Stuart slammed on the brakes and looked around for some potential catastrophe. "What in the world, Reese?"

"Look, Dad. Look on the corner. That lady. I think she needs a ride. She looks really cold. I'll crawl over in the back and give her my seat."

Stuart looked out his window. "That's thoughtful, Reese, but we're only going four blocks down the street to our house. That would hardly be worth the effort, don't you think? She knows where she's going." Stuart kept driving.

Reese tried again. "But, Dad, she's just standing there."

Jillian turned around to him. "Well, maybe she's waiting on someone, Reese. I'm sure she'll be just fine. And besides, that roast in the oven won't wait much longer."

Reese watched the young woman as long as he could see her. She sat down on the sidewalk bench and hovered over her bundle. The wind was blowing, but at least the sun was shining.

As they walked through the back door at home, Riley sniffed deeply. "Mmm! I can smell that roast and onions."

In a matter of minutes, the aroma of hot buttered rolls had mingling with the roast and vegetables as Jillian make quick work of browning them. She put all the food on the table, and Stuart picked Riley up and swung him around a couple of times before perching him atop a stack of pillows in his chair. On a regular Sunday the O'Hara boys would change clothes before they ate lunch, but not today. Jillian had already explained this Sunday's lunch was dress rehearsal for the family Christmas dinner just four days away.

Jillian sat down as Riley crowed with laughter. "Must you do that, Stuart? Remember what we're doing here. And I want to remind all of you that these ruby-red dishes have been in our family for three generations, and our goal today is that every one of them will be stacked back on the sideboard after we have eaten and cleaned up."

Stuart nodded in agreement and turned to his eldest son. "Reese, why don't you say grace for us today."

"Yes, sir." They bowed our heads, and Reese prayed. "Dear God, thank you for this food, because it's what we need to be healthy. Thank you that Dad has a job and that we have a warm house and this food to eat. And thank you that Mama is a great cook. And God, please bless that lady on the street corner. I think she needs you. Amen."

Reese noticed the momentary puzzled look on his mama's face, but the expression faded as she gazed at her family around her beautiful table, her pride emanating from her like a melody from a violin. She rose from her chair and walked around the table. "Napkins, everyone. Riley, sit up straight now, even though it's not easy sitting on those soft pillows, and let's tuck your napkin in just like I taught you." She stood beside Riley and let him wrestle with his napkin and then smoothed his red curls away from his shirt collar— the curls she kept saying should have been trimmed months ago. Reese knew his mom couldn't bear to see them gone.

"Riley, if you do well today and there's no gravy on you tie when you finish, you'll be ready for your own seat at the Christmas dinner table with the adults."

"But Dad has gravy on some of his ties," Riley quipped.

Stuart grinned. "Can't argue with that, Riley. Maybe I'll

join you at the children's table in the kitchen come Christmas."

Jillian responded quickly. "Remember, no children's table this Christmas." Sitting again, she began passing dishes to the left and everyone served their plates. Reese was on call to help his younger brother.

After a few moments during which everyone dove into their food with various expressions of approval, Stuart looked at Riley. "All right, Mr. Funny Guy, what did you learn in Sunday school today?"

Riley grinned. "Mr. Vince told us Jesus was born in Bethlehem in a manger."

Jillian dabbed at her mouth with her linen napkin. "But you already knew that. We read about that at home, and you'll get to see the live nativity tonight. So did you learn anything new?"

"Mr. Vince said Jesus was born in a house of bread."

Reese was quick to correct his brother. "No, Riley, Jesus wasn't born *in* a house of bread. That's just what *Bethlehem* means—"house of bread.'"

"Well, I wish I was born in a house of bread, especially if there's lots of butter and some of Mama's mayhaw jelly." Riley put more butter on his roll. "Oh, and then we found Baby Jesus."

Reese saw the slight grin on his mama's face and her glare giving him the you-better-not laugh look.

"Well, that certainly sounds interesting," she said.

Riley kept smearing butter and telling his story. "Mr. Vince and Miss Angie helped us all make crowns out of cardboard. We glued on sparkly stuff to make 'em look fancy, because we were going to be kings. Then Mr. Vince held up this tinfoil star on a stick, and we followed him all around the church, everywhere he went. He said, 'You have to be quiet,' but Melissa squealed real loud when we found

Baby Jesus. She hurt my ears. I don't know why she squealed. It was just a plastic doll. It was no Baby Jesus."

"I don't think that was the point, Riley. Anyway, I'm glad you know the story, and it will make this evening's live nativity and carol sing more meaningful to you."

Riley said, "I just hope Melissa got all her squealing done this morning. That girl can really squeal."

They kept eating, and nobody except Reese saw the gray-hooded woman in a brown trench coat carrying the red plaid bundle. He watched her walking slowly down the sidewalk and looking into their dining-room window as she passed.

After lunch, Riley wanted to play video games in his room, and Reese heard his dad say he would be in his home office getting a head start on his year-end reports. The afternoon sun stretched its fingers through near century-old windowpanes. When his mama curled up on the window seat like a cat to take a nap after she finished wrapping presents, he decided he'd go upstairs to do some drawing. Although he looked out the window more than once for the blond woman, he didn't see her.

———•———

Right after the grandfather clock in the foyer struck five, Reese heard his mama calling them downstairs. They put on their warmest sweaters and jackets and decided to walk the four blocks down Second Avenue to the church and save the parking places for visitors. Riley pitched a fit to wear his brown beanie with stuffed wool antlers sewn on each side, so their mama allowed it. After all, it was Christmas.

People were already gathering when the O'Haras arrived at the church. The pastor had made an announcement during the morning service, asking members to gather in the basement of the church for last-minute instructions. He handed out Christmas carol booklets while Mrs. Franklin made the announcements.

"All right, you good people. We've been working and waiting on this event for months, and it looks like we're going to have a great crowd on this beautiful evening. God smiled on us and calmed the wind. Now I invite you all to gather your family members and head outside to the manger scene on the front lawn of the church. You might want to keep a close eye on your little ones tonight. Lots of folks and lots of excitement, and we want all the excitement to be about the reason for the season, not because some chipper fellow decides to climb on the two-humped camel. And if you don't mind standing, that'll make sure some of our older folks and guests get the chairs. The handbells are ready to begin playing, so let's go make some noise for Baby Jesus."

Reese remembered that when he was Riley's age, the big Christmas event in Bar Haven had been the lighting of the Christmas tree out at the lighthouse, but they'd stopped doing that when the lighthouse ceased operations. He was glad his gramps had purchased the lighthouse. It belonged to his family now. In any case, Mrs. Franklin had been determined to create a new tradition—a live nativity and carol sing.

Reese and Riley stood right in front of their parents. Reese sang every note because he knew the words and liked to sing, but Riley mostly fidgeted, singing only the few choruses he knew because Christmas music had been playing in the O'Hara's house since Thanksgiving. Reese watched his little brother's green eyes follow the star dangling from the oak tree and bouncing from limb to limb in the breeze. Finally, the wind quieted and the star was still.

Reese felt Riley tugging on his jacket sleeve. Reese

looked down at him and kept singing "Star of Wonder, Star of Might, Star with royal beauty bright . . ."

Riley leaned forward, pointed at the manger, and whispered, "Look, it's Baby Jesus."

Reese nodded and agreed with him and just kept on singing, never missing a beat.

Riley was about to topple over, floppy antlers and all, as he pulled on Reese's sleeve again. This time, he whispered louder. "Look, Reese, it's the real Baby Jesus."

That's when Reese saw his mama yank gently on the red curls sticking out from under Riley's beanie cap and put her hand on his shoulder to keep him still.

Reese watched as Miss Irma stepped out of the group of carolers. Her husband was right behind her with a folding chair and an autoharp. Reese wasn't sure that folding chair was going to hold her up. He had heard Gramps say one time Miss Irma had a wide girth, but she took her seat beside the manger, placed the autoharp in her lap, and began strumming. Everyone in town knew this was the one night of the year she lived for—when the whole town listened to her. She probably had thoughts that the winds might even carry her voice out to sea where the sailors would be spellbound.

"Sweet Little Jesus Boy, born long time ago . . ." Miss Irma had been singing that song to the good people of Bar Haven far longer than Reese had been alive.

He felt Riley fidgeting, having no concern for Miss Irma's singing aspirations. Riley couldn't be stilled or silenced any longer. Just as Miss Irma sang, "Our eyes wuz blin', we couldn't see, we didn't know who you wuz," Riley broke loose from Jillian's grip, ran to the manger, and let out his own high-pitched squeal. "It's Baby Jesus, the real one. He showed up under the star for Christmas."

Reese watched the whites of Miss Irma's eyes grew larger

as she looked at Riley, and then she rotated her head to search the chorus of singers for Jillian. She sang louder over Riley's shrieking. Reese didn't know what to do.

"Look, everybody, it's really Baby Jesus," Riley squealed again and started jumping up and down, his stuffed antlers flopping from side to side. Then he froze. "Holy cow, there's two of them, and one of 'em is real. Really real." Then came the jumping up and down again.

Everybody was looking around at each other, peering over shoulders, and trying to see into the manger. Stuart raced around the behind the crèche and came in from the other side to get to Riley. Reese followed his dad and stood as he knelt and took Riley by his shoulders, trying to quiet him.

"Look, Dad. It's really Baby Jesus. He's moving. That's no plastic doll like Reese said."

Reese and his dad looked. Reese's jaw dropped.

"Oh, my, it *is* a real baby," Stuart choked out.

Miss Irma's voice was almost a whisper by now. "Sweet Little Holy Child, and we didn't know who You wuz."

Reese stood frozen while his dad crawled on his knees to reach into the manger. Riley was right at his elbow, looking over their dad's shoulder. When Stuart took the baby in his arms, the baby started crying.

"See, Dad, I told you it was the real Baby Jesus. I knew it was Him, but I didn't know Baby Jesus cried."

By now, everyone was realizing just what was going on. As Miss Irma strummed the last chord, Pastor Franklin made a beeline to the manger and helped Stuart stand up. An excited murmur rose from the crowd.

"Well, Riley," said Pastor Franklin as the three of them turned to face everyone. "I'm glad you recognized the baby, and I'd say this Baby Jesus stole the show." Everybody started clapping and looking at each other, and then things got quiet.

The pastor seized the moment. "Is the mother of this beautiful child here?" Everyone looked around to see if anyone would claim the baby. No one did. The pastor whispered something in Stuart's ear.

No one paid attention to the young woman in the brown trench coat at the back of the crowd, but Reese saw her. He watched her walk away into the darkness.

Stuart took Riley's hand and started toward the side door of the church. He nodded at Jillian and Reese and motioned for them to join him as Mrs. Franklin led the group in singing the last carol, "Joy to the World."

They had barely gotten to the pastor's study when Mrs. Franklin came rushing in like the building might be on fire. She removed her coat and tossed it across her husband's desk chair. "Here, Stuart, let me see that child. I have three sons and a whole herd of grandchildren. I don't know much, but I know what to do with a baby."

Stuart gladly gave the now squalling infant to Mrs. Franklin. Reese and Riley stood beside their dad, lined up like choirboys, and just stared at that bundle she was holding. Jillian stepped to Mrs. Franklin's side and eased the blanket away from the baby's face.

"Oh, its little cheeks are so red, probably from the wind and cold. Oh, Rosemary, I sure hope it's not from fever."

"Me too. Grab a pillow over there, and let's put him down."

Jillian grabbed the green chenille pillow from the sofa across the room and put it on top of the pastor's desk.

Mrs. Franklin gently laid the baby on the pillow and began to unwrap him just like he was her last Christmas present. "This is unbelievable," she said. "We haven't had a baby born in this parish in the last three months. I know Jenny Walton is in the family way, but her baby isn't due until March. I just don't understand it. If you don't want your baby these days, all you have to do is to leave it at the fire station, so who in the world would put a newborn baby in the manger outside on a night like this and just walk away? Something terrible is going on here. I feel it in my bones, and I have goosebumps."

Reese gently spoke up. "I know. I know who did it."

Mrs. Franklin stopped unwrapping her Christmas surprise. Reese felt all eyes turn toward him and sensed his face turning red like the baby's.

Stuart spoke. "Son, you don't know who the mother of this baby is."

"Yes, I do, Dad. I mean, I think I do."

Jillian leaned down and looked Reese in the eye. "Reese, you don't know any such thing. This is nothing to be joking about."

"I'm not joking, Mama. I know who she is. It's the woman in the brown trench coat. She was there in the back tonight."

Jillian turned to Mrs. Franklin. "I'm so sorry, Rosemary. I think Reese reads too much. He has quite the imagination."

"Mama, I'm not imagining this. I saw her."

Daddy put his hand on Reese's shoulder and turned him around. "What do you mean you saw her? Did you see her put the baby in the manger?"

Reese fumbled. "Yes, sir. I mean, no, sir. I mean, I didn't see her put the baby in the manger, but I saw her outside the church after the service this morning. She tried to go in but the door was locked." Reese grabbed the corner of the red plaid blanket. "See, she was holding something wrapped in this, but I didn't know it was a baby. And she was there tonight, like I said. But when Riley found the baby, I saw her walk away."

As Reese spoke, Riley got loose and squirmed between Jillian and Mrs. Franklin. With none of the adults paying attention to him, he reached the baby and started peeling away the plaid blanket and the thin flannel blankets underneath. Just as Reese was reminding his dad that they'd refused to give the woman a ride after church, Riley squealed again.

"Holy cow! I didn't know Baby Jesus was a girl. It's a girl. Look, Mama."

Jillian turned to see. "What? How do you know it's a girl?"

"She's dressed in pink, and she's got on a bracelet. She's smiling at me, and only girls smile at boys."

Before anyone could respond, Pastor Franklin walked in carrying a quilted bag. "Well, I called the police," he said. "They'll be here any second." He joined them around the desk to get a closer look.

Jillian started asking one question after another. "Why would a mother abandon her child? What will happen to the baby now? Who will take the baby home and take care of her?"

Reese stood quietly, watching the whole scene and listening. Spellbound, Riley never moved from in front of the bundle on the chenille pillow. He didn't respond until their mama asked the last question.

"We'll take her home, Mama. She's mine. I found her."

Jillian spoke softly. "She's not yours, Riley.

"When Dad found Lucky, we got to keep him."

Jillian stepped in. "Yes, Riley, but Lucky was a decrepit old dog. This is a baby."

"I know, Mama, but I take good care of Lucky every day. You know I do, and you know what we say—finders keepers."

The sudden opening of the door caught Reese's attention. Two police officers came in while as the adults in the room tried to convince Riley that "finders keepers" has nothing to do with discovering a baby in a manger on a cold night in December. Reese recognized Officer Davis but not the other one.

The baby began to cry again. Jillian picked her up off the pillow, red plaid blanket and all. "This baby's hungry. No way to know how long she's been lying in that manger. We need to get formula and some diapers."

Pastor Franklin raised the quilted bag he carried and looked at his wife and then the officers. "Maybe you should look in here. We found this stuffed in the manger after you left. Looks like a baby bag to me."

"Here, give me that." Mrs. Franklin took the bag from her husband, opened it, and started pulling out its contents. "Somebody who loves this baby came prepared. We have formula. We have diapers and wipes. We have medicine. And here're two envelopes. One of them says "To the good church people in Bar Haven."" She handed the pale pink envelope to her husband. "Here, see what it says."

The pastor removed the note and unfolded it, reading aloud.

I have left my baby with you because I have no other choice. I leave her with you because I love her so much and want her to have a good life. I thought you good people at the church would be the best ones to figure that out. I have no home, no responsible family support, little education, no steady job, and nothing to offer her but my truest love. That's why I leave her with you. Please keep the other envelope for my little girl and give it to her when she's old enough to understand. Please, please help her know I didn't abandon her. I did the only thing I knew to do. The letter will tell it all. It is my story and her father's. I pray God will be gracious to her.

Pastor Franklin looked at the second envelope. "There's a name here. Looks like the baby's name is Johanna."

Reese moved nearer his mama, who was crying by then.

Officer Davis looked at his watch. "Pastor, we have to call this in. This is child abandonment, and we have to get in touch with Child Protective Services."

Mrs. Franklin stepped in. "Just you wait a minute, Drew. It's Sunday night, and Christmas is coming in four days. You heard what this young mother said. She left the baby with us, the good people of the church. We'll find a way to take care of her until we can figure this out."

"I understand, ma'am, but that's not how this works."

"Drew Davis, do you remember when I coached your Little League baseball team?"

"Oh, yes, ma'am, I do. You were the only woman coach in the league. They nearly laughed us all out of town until that miracle of a season we had."

"Um-huh, I thought you'd remember that, Drew. Well, guess what. This is the Season of Miracles, and we're waiting on one. So why don't you just turn around and walk right out of here like we never called you. You understand?"

Officer Davis looked at Mrs. Franklin a moment, then the baby, then sighed and motioned his partner to the door. "No use arguing with the coach. But . . ." He stopped at the door. "I trust you, Ma'am. I know this baby will be well cared for in your hands. You have until the day after Christmas for your next miracle." With a quick nod, they exited the room.

Pastor Franklin smiled. "I've seen you in operation before, but tell us, Rosemary, what kind of miracle do you have up your sleeve this time?"

"No miracle, just plain old common sense. This woman here—" She waved the letter. "—loves this child, and she's going to stick around to make sure we did what she asked." She looked at Reese. "So, tell me, Reese. You've seen this young woman. You think you'd recognize her if you saw her again."

"Yes, ma'am. I think I would. Like I said, she had on a brown trench coat, and she was kind of small, and she had blond hair. She was parked in back of the church when we got here yesterday morning."

Mrs. Franklin looked dead straight at Reese. "That's good. Aren't you out of school for the holidays?"

Reese knew there was no backing down or out now. "Yes, ma'am."

"Good. I'll pick you up at eight thirty in the morning. We're going for a ride around town, out to the docks, and maybe over to the point. We'll find her."

Mrs. Franklin turned to Jillian. "Now, Jillian, do you want to take the baby home so that Riley can help you? Or do you want me to take her?"

Riley started his jumping-up-and-down routine again. "We'll take her. She's mine."

Stuart and Jillian looked at each other and just nodded their heads. Jillian said, "We'll take her, Rosemary."

Chapter Fourteen

Monday morning

The wind returned with Monday morning, and dark clouds smothered the horizon. Everyone was up early at the O'Hara house. The crying baby woke Reese, and he was quick to his feet to get ready. He had a sense Mrs. Franklin would arrive early. They had a job to do.

When he got downstairs, his mom was sitting next to the fireplace rocking the baby. "Dad already gone?"

"And good morning to you. Yes, we had an early breakfast. He built us a crackling fire and left for the office. It's the busiest time of the year for him with year-end reports for many of his clients, and he wanted to get as much done before Christmas Eve as he could."

Reese walked over and touched the baby's cheek. "Did the baby keep you up last night?"

"No. It wasn't the baby who kept me up. It was wondering how we're going to solve this problem. The baby slept peacefully but woke early and was hungry. Babies cry when they're hungry or need a diaper change or they're sick. At least, that was what you and Riley did. She seems to be happy after her bottle, so she's not sick."

"I heard her crying. That's what woke me. Do you think she misses her mom?"

"Oh, I don't know what an infant knows or thinks. I remember that I always thought you knew I was your mother. You seemed to be very contented when I was the one caring for you. If you don't mind, call Riley down. It would help if you boys could just fix yourselves a bowl of cereal this morning."

Reese went to the bottom of the stairs and whistled and called out to Riley. Riley was down the stairs quicker than a jackrabbit. "Where's the baby?"

"Mama's rocking her. Come on, we're having a bowl of cereal. I'll fix your favorite with some banana slices, but I need to hurry before Mrs. Franklin gets here."

Riley sprinted into the gathering room to see the baby. "Mama, what is her name? I forgot."

"Her name is Johanna."

He repeated it. "Can I hold her? I found her, and you let me hold her last night when we got home."

"Yes, you can hold her, but later."

Reese added, "After you eat your cereal. Come on. I'm about to pour the milk, and we don't like soggy cereal."

The boys finished their breakfast, and Jillian made good on her promise. She positioned Riley on the sofa beside her and was allowing him to hold the baby when the doorbell rang. "Reese, could you please get the door? More than likely, it's Rosemary."

His mama was right. Mrs. Franklin entered the back door with bags in both hands and one hanging from each shoulder. She began handing them off to Reese and headed toward the sofa to see the baby. "Baby supplies. Diapers. Formula. Baby wipes. Everything I could think of you might need. Pattie met me at the drugstore early this morning. She loaded me up and wouldn't let me pay a thing. The town's buzzing with the story of finding a baby in the manger last night. Even had a newspaper guy call from Savannah." She moved nearer the fire to warm herself. "This is one Christmas story if I ever heard one. I mean, besides the real one."

"It was quite a memorable first live nativity, wasn't it? I'm just so sorry Riley made such a fuss."

Mrs. Franklin rubbed her hands together and laughed. "It was perfect! Think about it. God's full of surprises, and what a surprise to find a real baby in the manger, only to discover it's a girl."

"Well, now that you put it like that . . ."

Reese was all ears as Mrs. Franklin continued reporting. "Pattie said there was a young girl with a baby in the drugstore Saturday afternoon, but she didn't recognize her. She looked through the receipts to see if she could find a name, but the girl must have paid cash. Pattie remembered her because she bought items the baby would need, and she bought a box of stationery. She said it caught her attention because no one buys stationery anymore. She had forgotten they even sold it."

Jillian commented. "The note she left was written on pink parchment with a matching envelope and the other envelope, the one she wrote for Johanna, was in the same kind of envelope. Sounds like Pattie has seen the girl too."

"Yes. And I spoke with Griff and Irma. Griff thinks he repaired the girl's car, and I got an earful from Irma about her conversation with this young woman in her café. She said the girl was of slight build and blond, but Irma doesn't think this girl would be giving up this baby. Puzzling, just plain perplexing. She has to be this baby's mother, but no one knows where she is."

Reese interrupted. "That's the same one I saw." He looked at his mama.

"Go ahead, Reese, tell her everything you know."

Reese expanded on what he'd told everyone last night, including having seen her leaving the church parking lot early Saturday morning when he and his father arrived to set up the nativity.

Rosemary asked, "Do you remember what kind of car she was driving?"

"Not really. It was a medium-sized car, and I think it was gray. Kinda old."

"Well, that's something."

Reese went on to report that he had also seen her after church on Sunday out on the bench in front of the church and that she'd walked up to the front door of the church, but it was locked. He described her brown trench coat over a hoodie that covered her head and the plaid blanket wrapped around the baby.

Rosemary shook her head. "What a sad day that we have to lock the doors of the church! And just when someone needed to come in."

"Yes, ma'am. She just walked away. I tried to get Dad to give her a ride, but we were in a hurry. And I saw her after that too."

He felt his mama's eyes. "Do you mean at the church?"

"No, ma'am. I saw her walking down the street."

"What street?"

"It was while we were having lunch, and I saw her out the window in the dining room. She was just walking down the sidewalk. And then she was there last night, and she had on the same coat. She was standing way in the back of the crowd. But she left in a hurry when Riley found the baby."

Mrs. Franklin adjusted her coat. "Let's go, Reese. We don't have any time to waste today. We're going to find this woman."

Jillian took the baby from Riley. "But I don't understand why you're so determined to find her. She obviously intends to give the baby up for adoption."

Rosemary pointed her finger at Jillian. "That's what you think. What's obvious to me is she's the one asking for help. She didn't leave her baby at the fire station or the police station or the medical clinic. There's a reason for that. She left her baby at our church."

"But still, she left her. She doesn't want her."

"Her note did not sound like she didn't want her baby. It sounded like she had no other option. By the way, what about the other note? Did you read it last night?"

"No. I didn't think I should. It was addressed to the baby."

"My sweet Jillian, I don't care whose name is on the envelope, we're not waiting eighteen years to find out what's in that note. It may give us a clue."

Reese said, "I'll get it, Mama. Is it in the baby's bag in your bedroom?"

"Yes, in the outside pocket."

Reese returned with the envelope and handed it to Rosemary. She opened it and began to read aloud.

My dearest Johanna, my gracious gift from God. That's what your name means, but I did not know that when I named you. You were the best of your father and me, and I gave you both our names. Giving you up was the hardest thing I ever have done, and I'm not sure I'll ever have anything but a broken heart. I never want you to think I left you because I did not love you. It was because I loved you so very much.

You see, I grew up in a house where anger and pain and little to no love lived. I was neglected and had to parent myself. Then I met your father, John, during my senior year in high school. He was a few years older. He worked at the grocery store where I worked part time after school. For the very first time in my life, I felt loved. He understood me because he grew up like I did, except that his mother truly loved him. But she died when he was a teenager.

We fell in love and were engaged and planning to be married. He took a job on an offshore oil rig to make money so we would have a good start. Our plan was for him to work for a few months and return home for us to get married. He was making good money and had learned how to weld. I was planning to go to nursing school. It was my dream.

But that dream, and all my dreams, died when your father was killed accidentally on the oil rig. His body was never found. A little after I learned of his death, I learned I was going to have you. Carrying you brought me such comfort in my sadness and grief.

You were born on October 10, 2003, and it was the happiest day of my life. I have loved holding you and thinking about the kind of person you will be. I think you will have your father's eyes and coloring. I know that every day from the day I write this letter, I will think of you and look for you in every young girl's face I see, but I pray I have done what is best for you. If only your father had lived, we would have done right by you, being better parents than we had. But I have only a high-school education, no one to help me, and I have no right to keep you when I cannot provide the things you need.

I was on my way to Hilton Head when circumstances sent me to Bar Haven. Maybe it wasn't circumstances at all. I'm praying God directed me there, because I think I have found a place where the people are good. If I leave you here, you will be taken care of and have wonderful parents. They cannot love you more than I do, but they can give you things I cannot. I know you will wonder about me and about your father, just as I will wonder about you. I'm praying that one day in heaven, you and your father and I will be together as it was supposed to be, and you will know us then. Never, never forget how much I love you.

Forever and always,
Your mother

Reese watched his mama wipe her eyes as she stared at the baby she was holding.

Jillian sniffled. "Oh my. I don't know what to think or to say."

Mrs. Franklin quickly added, "Like I said. She is desperate, and she needs help. And with God's direction, we're going to find her. We'll see to it she gets the help she needs. Then that baby will have a mother—her mother. Get your coat, Reese. Let's take a ride."

Canvassing the stores on Seaside Drive, Reese followed Mrs. Franklin as she went in every store to inquire if anyone had possibly seen a young woman fitting the description. She stopped at Irma's to ask if the girl had returned. She crossed the street to Griff's. He hadn't seen her since Saturday morning, but he said her name was Anna Beth and that she had spent some time in the library on Saturday. He gave Mrs. Franklin the description of the car and told her Anna Beth was interested in the lighthouse. That bit of information prompted Mrs. Franklin to drive out to the Point. Anna Beth was nowhere to be found.

After a day of riding and stopping to ask questions, Mrs. Franklin pulled into the driveway and dropped Reese off. "Well, Reese, I appreciate your being with me today. We learned more than we knew this morning, but unfortunately, no real results. Drew has given us until Friday to find her. I think if nothing else, we have the town stirred up, and everyone will be looking for her. If she's anywhere around, someone will spot her."

"Yes, ma'am. We did our best." He hesitated. "Maybe she'll come back. But my mom will take good care of that baby. You know she will."

"Yes, I do know that. Thank you again, and I'll see you Wednesday night at the Christmas Eve service."

Reese got out of the car and waved as Mrs. Franklin drove away. *The Christmas Eve Service.*

Chapter Fifteen

Christmas Eve

L ife with a baby in the O'Hara's house had changed things, especially with the Christmas preparation and Jillian's parents arriving. Jillian had not been equipped for a baby—no bassinette, no changing table, no car seat or clothing. But as things happen in Bar Haven, the church ladies brigade showed up with the needed items—some brand new and others retrieved from storage in attics. She accepted each gift graciously and assured the ladies all items would be returned when they were no longer needed.

She had many offers to help, but with Stuart taking on more responsibilities for the boys, she managed well. Balancing the care of a baby with all the Christmas preparation, Jillian found herself quite content with her boys and little Johanna in the house. All she'd ever wanted was to be a wife and mother, and she had longed for another child. Son or daughter, it mattered not. But it was not to be. She was grateful for the miracle two she had, but Johanna reminded her of how much she missed caring for an infant, from milk breath to the soft sighs of peaceful slumber to the fresh smell and touch of the infant's skin after a bath.

Rosemary either came by or called Tuesday with her offer to help, but she had no more news of the mother. In some strange way, Jillian was relieved. It wasn't that she didn't want Johanna's mother to be found, but she did hope it wasn't too soon. She gave instruction to herself as she warned the boys not to get too attached to the baby.

Drew had given them until Friday, the day after Christmas, to locate the mother. Then Children's Protective Services must be notified. They would take the baby into their care. Although Jillian had made no mention of it to Stuart or to Rosemary, she had already secretly checked into requirements for becoming a foster parent. Surely they would be allowed to keep Johanna until something more permanent could be settled. Time would tell. But for now, she had a couple of more days.

———•———

Jillian's parents arrived from North Carolina. It was not the Christmas Eve to which they were accustomed in Bar Haven. Gale winds were blowing, this time bringing in sheets and showers of rain. Church bells rang as families dashed into the church, folding their umbrellas, shedding their raincoats, and taking their seats for the candlelight service. The O'Haras took their normal third-row seats on the organ side. Unaware of the beautiful music, Reese watched as his mama held Johanna, seeming to enjoy every moment. But he recognized sadness in her eyes—a sadness in knowing she was only guarding a treasure belonging to someone else. Riley sat beside her and just stared at the baby. His grandparents sat next to Riley.

Reese had a notion that the woman in the brown trench

coat might show up for this Christmas Eve service if she were still in town. He'd told no one about his hunch, not even when he begged his dad to no avail to sit in the back. He'd explained that it would be easier for his mama to slip out if the baby started crying. What he'd really wanted was the better view sitting in the back would have given.

He fidgeted and swiveled in his seat between his parents for the first forty-five minutes, watching. No sign of her.

It wasn't until the service was almost over, and the congregation was singing the last chorus of "O come to my heart, Lord Jesus. There is room in my heart for you" that Reese turned one last time. Someone stood in the shadows just inside the doorway. Someone in a brown trench coat and with blond hair that looked like spun gold in the candlelight. It was Johanna's mother. *I knew she'd come.*

Reese felt his heart beating as though he was on the swimmer's block, waiting to dive into the water when the starting pistol fired. He nudged his dad. "She's here," he murmured. "Johanna's mother."

His father kept singing but his eyes asked the question. Reese nodded toward the back. "Standing just inside the doorway."

Stuart leaned to whisper to Reese. "I'm going to her. Stay here and tell your mama what's happening and that I'll be in the pastor's study." He quickly exited the pew and headed toward the back of the sanctuary.

Reese couldn't wait until the service was over. With a quick explanation to his mama, he slid out of the pew and joined his dad. Stuart had taken the young woman's arm and led her into the vestibule where he could speak to her. "Hello, Anna Beth. That is your name, isn't it?"

Reese saw that she was startled.

"Yes, sir." She bit her lip.

Reese couldn't hold back. "I knew it was you. We have

Johanna. She's staying with us."

Anna Beth began to cry and nearly crumpled to the floor. Reese followed his dad's lead and took her other arm. They led her to the pastor's office where she could sit and they could talk privately.

Amid her whimpering, she asked, "Is my baby okay?"

Stuart answered. "Yes, she is fine. She has been with us since Sunday evening." He paused. "Look, you're not in any trouble. We know something about you from the notes you left, and we know you love your baby. You were just desperate. We only want to help you."

Reese had never seen such a searching look in anyone's eyes. "My dad's right," he spoke up. "We've been looking for you. We looked everywhere. My mama and Mrs. Franklin just want to help you, and my dad does too."

———•———

The amen of the benediction was still resonating in the church when Jillian, Riley, her parents, and Mrs. Franklin burst through the door of the pastor's office. The pastor joined them as soon as the last parishioner had wished him Merry Christmas.

Anna Beth was seated on the sofa with Reese on one side and Stuart on the other, but they moved quickly and allowed Jillian to sit with her and place the baby in her arms. Sniffling and with tears rolling from her cheeks, she held her baby close. She was unable to speak.

Mrs. Franklin sat down on the other side of her. "Gentlemen, I think it might be a good thing if you left the room and let us ladies have a little talk. Why don't you all go and lock up?" She waited until they left the room and closed the door, then said, "Anna Beth, we are so glad you returned."

Jillian nodded in agreement.

"My name is Rosemary Franklin. I'm the pastor's wife, and this is Jillian O'Hara. She's been taking care of your precious baby since we found her Sunday evening."

Anna Beth looked at Jillian. "Thank you. I just had to come back to see if Johanna was okay. I don't know what else to say."

Rosemary answered. "That's okay, because I do know what to say. We know a little of your story from the notes you left with the baby. We know it has been a most difficult time for you these last several months. You've been grieving, and at the same time trying to give care to this precious child. And the hardest part is that you've been alone to make major life decisions all by yourself. Am I right?"

Anna Beth was able to eke out a faint, "Yes, ma'am."

"Look, my young friend, most of the folks I know have had some rough patches in their lives, but around here, we stick together and we help each other out until things get better. And we don't want you to be alone. We only want to help you."

Anna Beth broke down. "But why would you want to help me?" she asked between sobs.

"Why wouldn't we want to help you? Last time I checked, there was no list of requirements you had to meet to get some help."

"But this is a church, and I am an unwed mother, and I was willing to give my baby away."

Jillian answered before Rosemary could speak. "We want to help you because we *are* the Church, dear. That's what we *do*."

Rosemary added, "Jillian's right. And I seem to remember a story about another unwed young girl—the one God chose to bear His son because He saw something special about her. I believe He chose you to be Johanna's mother, and I also believe that you showed sacrificial love in wanting your baby to have the very best life she could have. And you don't think you can provide that. You didn't want to give your baby up because you didn't want her. Am I right about that too?"

Jillian handed Anna Beth a tissue.

"Yes, ma'am." Anna Beth's voice cleared. "John and I were engaged to be married, but he was killed. I just finished high school and only had a part-time job at a supermarket. Childcare took just about all the money I made, so I was on my way to Hilton Head where my mom is. But she said not to come. She wants nothing to do with me or my baby. I have no one and no means of making a living right now."

"But your letter said you were planning to go to nursing school."

Anna Beth held her baby close and rocked back and forth. "That was just my dream, and dreams don't come true. Besides, nursing school takes money too. I can't even feed my baby."

Rosemary eyed Jillian. "I do believe we can help with all of that."

Jillian joined her. "Of course, we can, and we will. Would you start by accepting my invitation to come home with us tonight? We just live down the street. I know that we're all strangers to you, but we're not strangers to each other in this town. I have two boys of my own, and they've grown to love Johanna in just three days. Would you come and spend Christmas with us?"

Anna Beth kept rocking and holding her baby. "If you're sure I wouldn't be too much trouble, then, yes, ma'am. I would."

"Well, then, let's get going. We don't need to talk anymore tonight. You just need some time in a safe place with your baby. We have a comfortable guest room with a private bath, and we have everything Johanna needs there except her mother. And tonight, that baby will have all she needs."

Rosemary added, "Jillian's right. No need to talk anymore. I'm a mother, too, and I leave early in the morning to be with one of my sons in Atlanta for Christmas, but I can assure you, there are no better folks than the O'Haras. You'll be well taken care of. Let's just enjoy Christmas, and I'll be back Saturday. We'll figure out the rest as we get to know one another. Is that okay with you?"

Rosemary stood and helped Anna Beth to her feet. "Are you strong enough to get yourself and the baby to Jillian's car, or do you want Jillian to take the baby?"

"No, ma'am. I mean, yes, ma'am. I can get to the car, but I'd like to hold my baby." She hesitated. "Everything I own is in my car, and it's parked out back. Is it okay to leave it here?"

Jillian answered. "That's no problem. If you will give me the keys, I'll get Stuart to drive it to our house. The boys can ride with him."

---·---

After a brief time of getting acquainted and joining the O'Haras—including the grandparents—for their bedtime snacks, Anna Beth was glad to be led to her room. She sat on the edge of the bed and held tightly to Johanna while Jillian and her mother moved some of the baby things into the guest room. Before they left, Jillian said, "If you need anything, I'm just down the hall. We want you to be comfortable and feel at home with us. I noticed you didn't eat much, so if you get hungry, there's plenty in the kitchen. And remember, you and your baby are safe here. We have some friends arriving from Tybee Island in the morning. And now you and your baby will be our special guests for Christmas. It will be a beautiful day."

Before Jillian could leave the room, Riley stepped through the door and walked to Anna Beth. "I have to go to bed now because Santa Claus is coming tonight. But Mama always lets me say goodnight to Johanna. She's kinda mine because I found her. I thought she was Baby Jesus. But I know Baby Jesus wasn't a girl."

Anna Beth smiled for the first time in weeks when she watched Riley lean to kiss her baby's cheek. Riley touched the soft fuzz on the baby's head. "You better go to sleep, little baby. And when you wake up, you'll see what Santa Claus brought you."

Jillian chuckled. "That's my Riley. Your daughter and my son made our live nativity one we'll never forget, and now you have given us a most blessed Christmas Eve. We're so happy you're here with us. Good night." She was about to close the door when she turned to say, "You don't need to worry about oversleeping. Riley will be your alarm clock. He'll come barreling down the stairs early. We'd love for you to join us for our traditional Christmas-morning breakfast—Irma's famous sticky buns. Then we'll have a quite a spread for our Christmas lunch. You can get better acquainted with everyone and the house tomorrow. Right now, you just get some rest." Jillian closed the door.

Anna Beth sat in the warmly lit silence and peacefulness of the room. It was Christmas Eve, and she was in a house with strangers who felt more like family than she had ever known, except with John and Miss Edith. How could she be so weary and so hopeful at the same time? She still didn't have answers to what the future held, but this night and these people had given her a sense that all could be well. Even more than that, they were more reminders to her that God was indeed gracious.

For the first time since Johanna's birth, Anna Beth slept peacefully with her baby next to her. It was almost Christmas. Not the Christmas she and John had dreamed of, but she had her baby, and she wasn't alone.

Chapter Sixteen

———◆———

Christmas Day

T he storm and winds had passed during the night. The skies were still velvety dark when the O'Hara house came alive, but within an hour, the Christmas-morning sun was shining through every window in the house.

The boys were still in their pajamas and unwrapping gifts, and Jillian, Stuart, and her parents sat in their bathrobes sipping coffee, licking the sticky off their fingers, and enjoying the boys' delight at every package opened. Jillian was disappointed that Anna Beth had not appeared, but she never once cautioned the boys to be quiet. Her living room pulsated with pure joy, and she wasn't about to ask them to turn the volume down.

Riley jumped up from the floor where he was going through the pieces of his fort builder and asking Reese to help him. He was the first to see Anna Beth. "Come on, little baby, you gotta see what Santa left for you. And I gotta show you what I got. I'm going to build us a fort."

Jillian turned to see Anna Beth fully dressed along with

the baby. Jillian went to her and invited her into the room. "Oh, you look so lovely this morning, Anna Beth. And look at you, Johanna. You look like a Christmas angel. I'm sorry I forgot to tell you we'd be in bathrobes."

"That's okay."

"Let's get you to the kitchen and get you a sticky bun. You haven't ever had one like Irma makes them. And I have everything ready for Johanna too." Jillian motioned for her mother to join them.

Jillian's mother took the baby and fed her while Anna Beth drank her coffee and enjoyed her bun and joined in the conversation.

"This bun is delicious. I actually ate at Irma's last Friday while Mr. Griff was repairing my car."

Jillian poured herself another cup of coffee. "Yes, we heard all about that. You already have friends in this town, and that beautiful baby has already won lots of hearts."

Anna Beth's smile delighted Jillian.

"They were both really nice to me." Anna Beth paused. "I have to tell you something. It's important to me. I don't want you to think I was careless just leaving Johanna in the manger. I timed it to make sure she was fed and was sound asleep, and I hid in the trees to watch her until the crowd arrived. I thought there would be lots of good people at the church that night. It was just that everyone I met here was so helpful and welcoming. That's why I thought Johanna would find a good family here."

Jillian's mother quipped, "Oh, this little one already has a good family, and it's you."

"Mother's right. She's always right." Jillian chuckled. "Just wait until you see what's under the tree for the baby."

"Oh, I hope you didn't—"

Jillian interrupted. "No, we didn't buy all the gifts. Like I said, your baby already has lots of friends here. Why, she's the town darling. Her friends have been dropping off presents for her since Monday morning. Most of the gifts left now under the tree have her name on them. Let's go see."

"That's a lovely tree there in the corner."

"Thank you. We put the fabulous tree in front of the living-room window for the town to enjoy. But this tree's my favorite. It's our family tree, and every ornament is handmade and has a story to go with it." She led Anna Beth to the tree and pointed out the ornaments Gramps had stored away. "I just found these a few weeks ago out in the carriage house apartment where Gramps—that's Stuart's father—lived. Gramps' father built this house, and he had lived here all his life. But when Gramps' wife died, he didn't want to live in this big house, so he gave it to us, and he moved out back to live in the carriage house. I was going through some things out there a few weeks ago, and I found all these hand-painted ornaments his mother made for him. So, we've added them to our family tree this year. It's our first Christmas without him."

"That's quite a tradition. It's the kind of thing John and I planned to do since neither of us had anything like that growing up."

Jillian could hear the wistfulness and the melancholy in Anna Beth's voice and put her arm around her. "I am so sorry, Anna Beth, that your life has been so difficult. I know this isn't the Christmas of your dreams, and it's your first without John."

Jillian's mother left the gathering room with the baby.

Anna Beth wiped her eye. "I am the one who is sorry. I shouldn't be bringing my sadness into your Christmas Day. I don't want you to think I'm not grateful. You have taken care of my baby and now you've invited us to have Christmas with you. And I really do thank you for everything."

"You are welcome. We're glad to help." Jillian was amazed at Anna Beth's maturity, her other-centeredness, and yet her childlikeness. "Let's dry those eyes and join the family. Maybe that'll lift your spirits a bit. I haven't opened my present from the boys yet. And Riley keeps telling me that it's something really special." She took Anna Beth's hand and led her to the living room. "That boy has such a hard time keeping a secret. I'm surprised he hasn't already told me exactly what it is."

They joined the family in the living room where Riley had another few pieces of what looked like over-sized Tinkertoys put together into a huge box. Reese was going through his new box of paints and brushes.

"Riley," Stuart said, "we have all afternoon to build a fort, and I think a better place to build it is in your room, and maybe your mama will find you an old sheet once you get the frame built. Would you please take it apart now, and put the pieces back in the box? Johanna hasn't seen what was left under the tree for her."

With one fell swoop of Riley's arm, the pieces lay scattered on the floor, and Reese helped him put the sticks and joints back into the box. "Don't forget the pictures and instructions, Riley. We'll use them later."

"Got it." When the floor was clean, Riley turned to Anna Beth, seated on the sofa with the baby. "You got to get down here on the floor, Anna Beth. That's where all the presents are. She can lie on her stomach, but Mama says not for long."

Anna Beth joined Riley on the floor. When Reese started to hand her the first presents, she smiled. "Riley, would you mind opening these gifts for Johanna. You can show them to her while I hold her."

"Heck, yeah."

Jillian cleared her throat to get her youngest's attention.

"I mean, yes, ma'am."

There were more than a dozen unwrapped boxes when Riley finished. Jillian could tell that Anna Beth was a bit overwhelmed.

"See," she said. "I told you your daughter had already made friends here."

"I see that she's made some really nice friends. It's her first Christmas, and you have made it a happy one for us both."

Jillian, wanting to lighten the moment, stood. "Look, everyone has opened a present except me. When do I get this present that Riley's been telling me about?"

Reese pinched Riley's ear. "Did you tell her, Riley?"

Riley put his hand over his ear. "I didn't. I just said it was special 'cause we made it."

Reese handed the large box to his mama. "Riley wrapped it."

"Thank you, Riley. My favorite color: green." She opened the box. When she saw what lay inside, her eyes widened and her jaw dropped. She pulled the board carefully from the tissue paper that held it. "Reese, did you really paint this?"

"Yes, ma'am. I was just going to paint you two doves to look like Gramps' Christmas ornament that you liked. But then you said you wanted to name the carriage house Dove's Landing, so Riley and I painted the sign, and Dad helped us attach the limb with the doves to the sign."

"It is perfect. Really perfect." She held it up for everyone to see. "Oh, Stuart. We'll get this hung this afternoon. I'd like it right above the door."

He smiled. "Consider it done. And if I recall, there's one more present to be opened."

Jillian returned his smile. "You're right. Do you have it?"

He patted his sweater pocket. "I do. It's right here." He handed the small box wrapped in gold foil to Jillian.

"Anna Beth, we have something for you. We didn't know that you would be here for Christmas, but we're so glad you are. Stuart and the boys and I have talked it over, and we would really be happy if you would accept this." She handed the box to Anna Beth.

Anna Beth slowly opened the box. She lifted a key ring that looked like a souvenir from a giftshop. It was a lighthouse that looked much like the one out on the point, and it had one key attached. She held it up.

Stuart said, "The key ring probably doesn't suit your tastes. When my father bought the lighthouse out on the point, there were boxes of these in the welcome area. It was the only one we had at home."

Jillian could see the questioning in Anna Beth's face. "It isn't the key ring that we're giving you. It's the key. We have talked and decided we want to make Dove's Landing available to you for as long as you need it." She ruffled Riley's hair. "Dove's Landing is our carriage house apartment out back. It's perfect for you and Johanna."

"You mean you want me to stay here?"

"Yes. Like I told you, Gramps lived in the apartment, and it's been sitting empty. Stuart and I have been talking about having someone live there. I've just repainted and gotten new furniture. It has everything you need. And now, thanks to my wonderful sons, it will even have a sign above the door."

Riley almost squealed. "You gotta stay, Anna Beth. I can help take care of the baby."

Anna Beth's blue eyes filled with tears. "I don't know what to say. You don't even know me, and you want me to stay in your apartment?"

Jillian joined her on the floor. "We know you well

enough. And we don't want you to just stay in the apartment. We want you to live there because we have some other ideas too. Like a part-time job. Irma needs help, and Griff needs help too. You could work part time, go to nursing school part time, and we can help with Johanna."

"You want to help me with all that?"

"We do. We don't have it all figured out yet, but that will come with time. We just know that God has been so gracious to us. We have this spacious home, and we decided it was a shame for the apartment to be empty. And just when we were thinking about all of that and getting the apartment ready, God provided you to come and live here, if you'd accept our invitation."

"Thank you." Anna Beth held tightly to the key in her hand as tears rolled down her cheeks. "Thank you so much. I promise I'll never be a bother." She closed her eyes.

Jillian heard Anna Beth's whisper. "I'm beginning to believe God is gracious."

———·———

It was late on Christmas night. Anna Beth could see from the front window of the carriage house apartment that the lights were off in the main house. It had been better than a good day with a real family and their friends, the Lamberts. Mrs. Lambert had brought dishes that tasted like Irma's cooking. The Lamberts were staying overnight. The house seemed to have room for everyone—family and friends. She imagined them all sleeping after a full day of celebration, great food, and then helping her move in. Before leaving the O'Haras' house after a light supper and walking over to the carriage-house apartment, she had told them that this day was the best Christmas she had ever had. And it truly had been.

Anna Beth walked out of the bedroom where little Johanna lay sleeping. Stuart, Jillian, and the boys had unloaded her car and moved all the baby things over to the apartment that afternoon. It all left her still trying to process and grasp their goodness. Her baby had her own room with a real baby bed, a changing table, a mobile of butterflies above her head, a chest filled with new clothes and bath linens, and a six-foot-high stack of disposable diapers. And Anna Beth had her own bedroom right down the hall.

She walked around the apartment that already felt like home. Shadowboxes showcasing gloves and lace-trimmed handkerchiefs and a shawl from three generations ago lined the wall in the hallway. Her eyes followed the artful calligraphy on the cards in each shadow box—notes that told a family story. Blueprints of the original house were framed and hanging over her bed, and a number of Reese's framed seascapes hung in appropriate places. She looked around the apartment whose walls and furnishings told stories of this family—a real family, the family who'd built this home and loved and lived here for three generations.

Anna Beth went into her bedroom, where all her belongings lay stacked in boxes. She would get to those tomorrow, but she had something she must do before she went to sleep. She found the box of pink stationery and a pen and settled into the lounge chair in the living room.

Dear Miss Edith and Mr. Harry,

I am sorry that I haven't written or called you to wish you a Merry Christmas. I want you to know that I have had the very best Christmas of my life. When I left Jacksonville last week, I could never have imagined all the things that have happened to me in the last few days.

I never made it to Hilton Head. After I left you, I

drove for more than an hour and stopped at a rest stop to call Mom only to learn that she and Rodney were having trouble and she didn't want me to come. All I knew to do was to return to Jacksonville, but my car wouldn't crank. A stranger, an older man named Josh, helped me get it started and told me about Mr. Griff in Bar Haven who would fix my car. So I drove there and got my car repaired. I want to thank you for the money you gave me. It paid for the repairs with some left over.

It's a long story, Miss Edith, and I want to see your face when I tell you every detail, but I was so desperate I was ready to give Johanna up. When I walked around this town and met some people, I knew it was the kind of place where Johanna could have a family and she would grow up safe and loved. I can't wait to tell you everything that happened. You won't believe it! But the best part is that the O'Hara family offered me their carriage-house apartment. And they want to help me go to nursing school, and Miss Jillian says she will take care of Johanna while I get a part-time job and go to school.

Oh, and Miss Edith, the whole family sat around a big table with the best food for Christmas lunch. We ate off real dishes, and they passed the food around and helped their plates, and they had such pleasant conversation. It was like how John and I wanted our lives to be.

I don't quite understand all that has happened yet, and we don't have all the details about school and work ironed out either, but I know there are good people in the world. People like you and Mr. Harry and Mr. Stuart and Miss Jillian. People who care about somebody besides themselves. I'll try to come and visit you soon and tell you the whole story.

But Miss Edith, I couldn't go to sleep tonight without telling you something. All those times you told me God is gracious, I wanted to believe it. Now I know it's true. God gave Johanna and me the best Christmas ever, a real Christmas miracle.

Love,
Anna Beth

She read over the note, folded it, and tucked it into the envelope. *I'll mail it tomorrow.*

Tomorrow.

For the first time since her dreams died with John, she liked thinking about tomorrow.

Epilogue

———◆———

Christmas 2020
Bar Haven

Looking back, I can tell you the Christmas of 2003 was the merriest of Christmases at the O'Hara house. Not a loud, boisterous time—other than Riley—but one of quiet joy. It was the Christmas that changed our family forever. There has been a little one in the O'Hara's house every Christmas since then.

You see, Johanna and her mother, Anna Beth, were our Christmas guests, but they became family. Anna Beth gratefully accepted the key to Dove's Landing, and she and her daughter lived there for three years. Mr. Griff hired Anna Beth part time to keep up with his parts inventory and his financial records, and Miss Irma hired her to work at the café when she had time. Anna Beth learned many of Miss Irma's secrets and cooked many a fine meal for us.

The best part was that Mr. Lambert was on the board of the College of Coastal Georgia in Brunswick and was able to help Anna Beth realize her dream of going to nursing school. Mama kept Johanna, which meant she had a smile on her face all the time. Mama still loves babies. And Johanna got her nursing degree. She's married now and is nurse administrator in a big hospital in Savannah. And Johanna? Well, she's just about to start college herself.

Anna Beth's story was like many more Mama heard through the years. For the last seventeen years, she has made Dove's Landing a safe haven for six more girls with babies and stories like Anna Beth's. Mama treated those girls like her own daughters and their babies like her grandchildren. She provided a nest until they were ready to fly, and she loved them fiercely just like she loved Riley and me. When one flew the nest, she spruced up the apartment, prayed, and waited.

This will be the first Christmas that there won't be a baby here, but we could have one yet, because the apartment is ready, and Mama's been praying again.

All her little birds still show up the weekend after Christmas all these years later to put their baby's first Christmas ornament on the family tree and to celebrate a Dove's Landing Christmas. Johanna was the only one of the babies that didn't get her ornament. But I have a surprise for Johanna this Christmas—a hand-painted ornament of a baby wrapped in a pink blanket lying in a manger. And underneath in bright gold letters: Johanna's First Christmas. And I painted a special ornament for Mama too—two doves on a limb with white letters: Dove's Landing's First Christmas, 2003.

About the Author

Phyllis Clark Nichols's character-driven Southern fiction explores profound human questions using the imagined residents of small-town communities you just know you've visited before. With a strong faith and a love for nature, art, music, and ordinary people, she tells redemptive tales of loss and recovery, estrangement and connection, longing, and fulfillment ... often through surprisingly serendipitous events.

Phyllis grew up in the deep shade of magnolia trees in South Georgia. Born during a hurricane, she is no stranger to the winds of change. In addition to her life as a novelist, Phyllis is a seminary graduate, concert pianist, and cofounder of a national cable network with health- and disability-related programming. Regardless of her role, Phyllis brings creativity and compelling storytelling.

Phyllis currently serves on a number of nonprofit boards. She lives in the Texas Hill Country with her portrait-artist, theologian husband.

Website: PhyllisClarkNichols.com
Facebook: facebook.com/PhyllisCNichols
Twitter: twitter.com/PhyllisCNichols